KILLER ENCORE

STELLA KNOX SERIES: BOOK SEVEN

MARY STONE
STACY O'HARE

Copyright © 2022 by Mary Stone

All rights reserved.

No part of this book may be reproduced in any form or by any electronic or mechanical means, including information storage and retrieval systems, without written permission from the author, except for the use of brief quotations in a book review.

❧ Created with Vellum

DESCRIPTION

In a psychopath's performance, revenge is the encore.

Moments after FBI Special Agent Stella Knox briefs the Nashville Violent Crime Unit on her father's murder, the teams' supportive camaraderie is replaced with horror when a stranger calls to tell Agent Martin Lin he'll never see his sister again.

A trip to Martin's apartment confirms the situation is real. Jane, who was visiting her brother, has disappeared without a trace.

As Stella and the rest of the team try to connect the dots between video footage showing Jane leaving a local liquor store before vanishing, their only clue is a bloody piano tuner. On the heels of their last murder case involving The Pianist, it seems like a bizarre coincidence.

But when Jane's body is found decapitated, accompanied by a grisly message for the FBI, it's clear this crime is personal. There's just one question...

Who's next?

Suddenly hurled into every FBI agent's worst nightmare, the entire team is soon embroiled in a deadly game of cat and mouse, where one misstep could mean the difference between life and death for the one they love.

Terrifying and adrenaline-charged, Killer Encore is the seventh book in the Stella Knox Series by bestselling author Mary Stone and Stacy O'Hare. Hang on tight, or you'll get thrown down a rabbit hole you never saw coming.

1

Jane Lin stood in East Nashville's Blue Label Liquor Store and tapped an impatient toe on the chipped linoleum floor.

Was this all they had?

The store's wine "section" consisted of six shelves crammed into the back of an outlet smaller than the vape shop under her New York apartment. Nashville's population was a tenth of New York's, but it still struck Jane that *someone* would want more than the four Woodbridge and Gallo wine options on offer.

She sighed.

She was visiting her brother, and he liked to talk a good wine game, sniffing the cork and scrutinizing the label. She'd seen him go on about "bouquets" and "hints of cedar" to Caleb, his best friend and FBI colleague, but luckily, he knew no more about the subject than she did.

And she knew that if you stuck a glass of white vinegar in front of him and said it was a thousand-buck Chardonnay, he'd call it crisp and zippy, saying it was the greatest thing to leave a spout since Aladdin polished some brass.

Not that she was any kind of wine connoisseur.

As a public defender, she couldn't afford the exotic vintages her old law school friends loaded into their upstate cellars by the crate. But even her local liquor store had choices—from Chardonnay to Chianti.

There was nothing in this store she couldn't find in the bargain bucket of a strip mall supermarket. Limited displays offered two kinds of vodka, four brands of light beer, all produced by the same beverage conglomerate, and a dozen types of whiskey.

Jane pondered selecting a whiskey instead of wine. This was Tennessee, after all. Martin might prefer it, but he'd ditched her tonight for his FBI colleagues.

However, she understood the nature of law enforcement, so she didn't begrudge him *too* much. Still, she'd come all the way from New York to see him.

Forget whiskey. I want wine.

She leaned back and called to the clerk sitting at the register, flicking at his phone. "Hey there, you got any Riesling?"

The clerk rubbed a palm against his thick black beard but didn't look up from his phone.

She raised her voice. "Hey, pal."

The clerk pulled an earbud from one ear. "Huh?"

"Riesling. Got any?"

He shook his head. "What you see is what I got." His Southern accent was so thick, it took him nearly a minute to get the sentence out.

Jane rolled her eyes and took a bottle of Pinot Grigio, wiping the dust from the shoulder of the glass with her thumb.

This stuff must have been sitting here since the days of the dinosaurs. Wine ages, though, right? The older the better.

At least that was what she'd heard.

She paid and left, her twelve-buck bottle hidden in a brown paper bag. Jane had tucked her wallet and phone in her back pockets to avoid carrying a purse on unfamiliar streets. Now, with only the wine in her hands, she felt like some kind of wino.

The area outside was empty. Every building across the street was dark. The only light came from the store itself, reddened by bottles of bourbon in the window. The glow hit the sidewalk, filtering through a metal grille covering the front of the store.

The building opposite looked like some kind of warehouse. A small window was high and unlit, so all Jane could see were three stories' worth of brick wall. An empty cigarette box crushed in the gutter and half-spilled bags of cement suggested someone was trying, and failing, to improve the place. Her brother's apartment was about a seven-minute walk away, on a street only slightly better than this one.

"Dude, gotta say, thought you'd be doing better," Jane muttered to herself.

She hadn't visited Martin since he'd been posted to Nashville three years ago. Her clients kept her in the city and his cases kept him too busy to meet up. But she'd managed to come down anyway, seizing hard-earned personal time. Even if Martin worked all day, Jane figured they could squeeze in a weekend of cozy meals and maybe even a bit of country music. That wasn't usually her kind of thing, and it had never been Martin's...but when in Rome and all that.

Maybe she should pick up a pair of cowboy boots while she was down here, to learn how to do a barn dance or something like that.

The thought made her laugh.

How her brother wound up down South and not in his beloved New York City was a mystery.

He must really love his work.

Retracing her steps, she turned toward his apartment and crossed in front of a dark alley, giving it a wide berth. As she was passing the next building, a shuttered storefront, she heard something.

Jane stopped. What was it?

"Help. Help me. Please."

A woman? Or maybe a child or young man? The voice was so faint.

The voice came from somewhere behind her. She turned but couldn't see anything.

"Help." The voice was even weaker this time. "Plee-ease."

Jane took a step back in the direction of the liquor store, her bottle gripped in one hand like a club. All her attention was on the dark alley. "Hello?"

"Mommy?" The voice definitely belonged to a child, and though Jane wasn't a mother, every maternal instinct inside her stood to attention.

She stopped at the mouth of the alley and peered inside. The passageway was just wide enough to hold a rusty dumpster. Stinking, rotting vegetables and the heavier stench of human urine permeated the air. Jane took half a step back, gripping her wine bottle tighter. The firm glass under the brown bag offered cold comfort.

Something rustled on the other side of the dumpster. Jane's heart thumped in her chest.

What the hell is that?

She tried to shake the fear out of her head.

C'mon, girl. A Tennessee raccoon's got nothing on a New York rat.

She took one step toward the alleyway, her feet still planted firmly in the middle of the sidewalk. "Hello? Is anyone there?"

The rustle came again, something moving against a

plastic bag. There were no words this time, only the sound of a young child crying.

Jane swallowed.

If that is *a raccoon, it'd better be no bigger than a rat.*

She inched forward. "Hell—"

"Mommy?"

The voice came from behind the dumpster. Gripping the bottle, Jane squeezed into the alley, taking care not to let her jeans touch either the dumpster or the wall. Although the weather had been hot and dry, the ground under her feet was wet and slippery. In spite of her sneakers, she had to move carefully to avoid sliding.

Reaching the other side of the dumpster, surrounded by the scent of rot, she pulled her phone out of her back pocket. In the beam of bright white light, a teetering pile of full trash bags climbed the wall. The leaning tower hovered over Jane's five-foot-five frame and stretched to the end of the alley.

She scanned the light over the garbage.

Thin coils of aluminum and sheets of dirty linoleum rolled out of some of the bags. The industrial smell of rubber and glue added to the stench of vegetables and urine. She brought the light down to the ground.

The lower half of someone's leg with dark blue or black pants and a black combat boot poked out between two giant black trash bags. The boot seemed incredibly small, almost like a child's.

"Dammit."

Jane lifted her phone. The light shone on a dark-haired person with pale skin, half-buried in the wall of garbage. She dropped onto her haunches and dragged one of the bags away. The person, whose sex or age she still couldn't distinguish, lifted a hand to protect their eyes against the phone's glare.

Not a child after all.

Jane lowered the light, casting everything in shadow again.

"Sorry. Are you okay? Don't move. I'll call for help."

The figure half rose, their face still hidden in the alley's shadows.

"No. Please. No ambulance. No police." The person's voice was both wispy and hoarse.

Jane still couldn't tell if it was a woman or a young man. "No police? But you're hurt."

"Please. Please, no."

Jane hesitated. "I can't just…tell you what. I'll call my brother. He's FBI. He'll know what to do."

She found Martin's number.

But as her thumb hovered over the call button, the shadowy figure shifted onto their feet. The move was so sudden and graceful that Jane fell back.

Before she could say a word or even lift a hand, her attacker swung, bringing up something heavy from the garbage pile.

An explosion, sickening and hot, thundered through Jane's head.

Dizzy and dazzled, she fell face-first onto the pile of garbage. The pain in her head throbbed and spiderwebbed from the base of her neck to her forehead and down her face. She saw the figure pick up her phone before the alley turned black.

MINUTES or maybe hours or days later, Jane blinked. The act made little difference to her vision.

Wherever she was, not even a slit of light peeked from under a door or through a window. Her head pounded, and her arm ached where it'd been pinned beneath her weight.

She pushed herself up. A wave of nausea gripped her. Vertigo.

Debris stabbed into her palms, as though she'd fallen asleep in a room carpeted with Legos. She winced. As she leaned back, her shoulder brushed a wall. Slightly relieved to have some support, she rested her back against it as she stretched her legs.

"Ow."

Every time she moved, her temples compressed, as though her head were in a vice, and someone was tightening and releasing it, only to retighten it again. She closed her eyes and swallowed hard. The back of her head felt cold.

When she touched her hair, a bolt of electricity shot from the nape of her neck across her face. Her hand returned sticky. She wiped her palm on the side of her jeans and felt in her pocket for her phone.

Gone. Of course it was gone.

She opened her eyes.

A wall of black.

Easy, now. Easy.

Her breathing slowed.

Jane forced her eyes to remain open, to allow her vision to adjust to the gloom. She held her breath, trying to listen. Silence greeted her. But there was always the possibility her kidnapper was here. Hidden. Watching.

The idea caused goose bumps to rise on her arms.

Jane released her breath in a thin, soundless stream. She took another and listened again.

Still nothing.

Eventually, the room lightened up enough to have some dimension. High to her right, a strip of narrow windows ran across the wall, the kind that gave natural light to basements and cellars. But the sky outside was black, the glow no stronger than a gray haze cast by a clouded moon.

However long she'd been unconscious, it wasn't enough to push her into the next morning.

She exhaled slowly again and waited for her eyes to focus further.

Jane appeared to be sitting at the back of a small stage or raised platform that was littered with masonry and wood. In front of the stage, school chairs were scattered in a disorderly fashion—their plastic seats broken and their legs sticking up like brambles.

A cloud moved past the moon. The silver glow from the windows grew brighter. The walls to either side of her were decked out in graffiti that had been layered over what looked like musical notes or sheet music.

A music room. A small one.

Maybe a school? What the hell am I doing in a school? How did I get here?

The place felt empty. Sounded empty. Looked empty. Abandoned.

Jane risked moving and pushed herself to her feet, curiosity and confusion driving her movements.

Her head throbbed. She wobbled a little in the darkness. Waiting for the room to stop spinning, she told herself to take it slow.

She spoke aloud, as though the sound of the words could take her out of this hellscape and back to the real world. "There was someone. I went to help. I bent down and...ow."

Her hand returned to her scalp. A giant knot had formed under her hair, which was still sticky with dried blood.

She lowered her hand. "And why are you standing here waiting to find out, idiot?"

Jane staggered to the edge of the stage and carefully lowered herself to the floor. Using her outstretched arms for both balance and guidance, she began to move sideways.

Stray chair legs scratched at her skin. She scooted closer to the wall, feeling along until she reached an alcove.

A thin gap at the floor let warm, musty air blow in at her feet. Her grasping hands touched a metal handle.

The door. She'd found the door.

Her heart leapt. Everything was okay.

She would get out, find a phone, and call her brother.

Easy.

Her fingers curled around the handle and pulled.

The door opened an inch before stopping.

She'd pushed so hard, the muscles in her arms began to ache. Jane stumbled into the remains of one of the chairs behind her. Its leg poked her already injured head.

"Ow. Dammit!"

Cradling the back of her head, Jane stepped forward again.

Through a gap, she could just make out the shape of a board wedging the door shut. She threw her weight against it anyway. It rattled but didn't give. Again and again and again.

"Nooo." Jane gave up all pretense of silence. She shouted through the door. "Let me out, you asshole! You've had your fun. We're done! Open this door right now, and I'll forget pressing charges!"

Her cries faded into the darkness. Quiet returned.

She sank to the floor.

"Dammit." Jane took a deep breath, telling herself to calm down. "Martin. Martin will help me. He's in the FBI. They have to help me." Her voice was so weak with fear and worry, she could barely hear herself.

She closed her eyes. Her head throbbed.

The door rattled as the board was pulled free.

2

"*Your sister? Ha ha ha. Oh, honey, you're never going to see your sister again.*"

FBI Special Agent Stella Knox's mind whirled as the wispy, oddly pitched voice on Martin Lin's phone echoed through her head.

Only a moment before, the mood in her small loft apartment in East Nashville had been one of calm camaraderie. She'd finally told the other members of the Nashville Violent Crimes Unit everything she knew about her father's murder.

They'd all listened as she described Keith Knox's assassination and explained how her dad's partner and best friend, "Uncle Joel Ramirez," told her it had been a hit by dirty cops. They'd paid close attention while she explained how Joel—far from being dead as she'd thought for *years*—was alive and living in Atlanta under an alias.

For the first time since his death, Stella felt she had the support she needed. Now she could go to Atlanta, confront her errant "uncle," and get key information to bring her father's killers to justice.

She'd thought of her brother, who'd died of cancer soon after their father's death, as she recounted the tragic story of their father. It felt as if he were with her.

We're going to get him, Jackson. We're going to get the man who killed Dad.

Jackson's voice resounded in her head. *"You go, Stella. Slap those cuffs on him."*

She'd almost chuckled to herself.

But all that hope and excitement died in the face of Martin's strange phone call. Her brother's voice disappeared under, *"Your sister? Ha ha ha. Oh, honey, you're never going to see your sister again."*

Horror and concern consumed the apartment like smoke from a blazing fire.

"Put Jane on!" Martin screamed into the phone. "Who is this? Answer me *now*, dammit!"

But the caller had hung up.

Special Agent Ander Bennett stepped over and pulled the phone away from Martin.

What followed was a brief arm-wrestling situation as Martin kept yelling. "Jane! Let me talk to my sister!"

For a second, it looked like SAs Caleb Hudson and Chloe Foster were going to step in. Caleb, Martin's best friend, a tall Black man whose expressions could go from sunny to stormy the instant he spotted trouble, moved forward.

Chloe, a woman of action with a roundhouse kick to prove it, got halfway across the room before Ander took over the situation. That was probably for the best. Stella wasn't sure who Chloe would've kicked to stop the emotional upheaval going on...and she didn't want to find out.

Ander, who was older and stronger than Martin, managed to take the phone and get a hand on his friend's shoulder. "It's okay, man. Listen, Jane must've dropped her phone or something. Someone probably found it, called a number, and when you answered, decided to play a joke. She's probably back at your place now, waiting for you, and all kinds of pissed off she lost her phone."

Hagen Yates watched from a corner spot on Stella's bright red sofa, sipping his beer. Overt shows of emotion from other people didn't generally rattle him. "Or maybe *she's* playing a joke. Hoisting you with your own petard or something."

Martin was infamous for his practical jokes.

He'd once cling-wrapped an entire floor of men's room toilets. Another time, he'd rigged confetti cannons in Caleb's car. The noise of the cannons in the parking garage had even triggered security. They'd come in with guns out, only to find Caleb covered head to toe in glitter and paper. He was still finding tiny bits of paper in his car seats.

If Martin's sister was anything like him, a prank was certainly plausible.

But Martin's reaction told another story.

Stella saw the fear in his face. She pressed one hand over her aching side and cursed Boris Kerne again. Her busted rib and wrist were gifts from the crazy pianist—a killer they'd stopped just nine days ago. She'd jumped in front of a bullet to save Hagen. Luckily, the vest took the brunt of it, but it still left her with a cracked rib. And she'd broken her wrist trying to break her fall onto a stack of stereo speakers.

Martin glared at Hagen. His face turned red, and he shook Ander's hand off his shoulder.

Nope. Not a joke. He thinks this is real.

"If some lunatic had picked up her phone, *how* would they have called me? You think my sister's stupid enough to leave her phone unlocked? She's a *New Yorker*. Nothing is unlocked."

"Wouldn't that make a joke more probable, then?" Hagen

countered. "If she's there, she could've just handed the phone to some rando and told them what to say."

"I know Jane. She might change your sugar to salt or wrap your toilet seat with cling wrap, too, but she'd never play with life and death. We're a law enforcement family. There are lines. Trust me, my sister's in trouble."

Hagen put down his beer and nodded. He must have felt the same tingle of trouble Stella did. In spite of his clean-cut features and style of dress, Hagen knew darkness. He could recognize a crisis.

Because of his passion for stopping criminals, she'd relied on Hagen's help with her father's case, even though the handsome agent had his own reasons for getting involved. His own father had been murdered. Since Memphis, Tennessee wasn't a *huge* city, they'd run on the assumption that their fathers' deaths—both drug-busting related—were probably connected.

They'd both have to wait to move forward, though. The immediacy of Martin's situation was too great.

And Stella wanted to support her team as much as they supported her.

She looked past Ander to the white-blond young woman sitting next to Hagen on the sofa. Mackenzie Drake was the best forensic cyber expert Stella had ever met. Mac didn't just know how to drill through data to find information. She also had an ability to look for intel they didn't even know they needed. That was a much rarer skill.

"Mac, can you get a location for Jane's phone?"

Mac eased herself to her feet. Almost two weeks ago, she'd been abducted and tortured by a mission-driven murderer. Physically, she was almost recovered. Mentally, who knew?

Special Agent Dani Jameson, who had been with Mac during that terrible ordeal, had gone on immediate maternity leave and had delivered a healthy baby girl. But Mac had come racing back, keener to spend time in the office with her colleagues than recuperating at home. Maybe she felt safer in the company of her coworkers.

Stella wasn't too sure what unseen bruises Mac was hiding.

Mac pulled out her phone and crossed toward the kitchen, where Chloe had retreated to perch on a high barstool. "Sure. Let me just make some calls."

Caleb sat on the arm of the sofa. "Where did you say Jane was going?"

He and Martin had become close friends since Martin had arrived in Nashville three years ago and were often joined together on fraud or organized crime task forces. Stella hadn't had an opportunity to work directly with them in the field yet.

Martin dropped his head into his hands. He talked through his fingers. "The liquor store. The Blue Label. You know the one. The crappy little place around the corner? She wanted to get a bottle of wine for the evening. I told her we didn't have much in the neighborhood, but she didn't care. She just wanted something white with alcohol in it and a cork."

Mac sat on the barstool next to Chloe and dropped her phone on the counter. "No dice. Her phone must be off."

Stella pushed her beer bottle to one side. She'd decided. They couldn't sit here and wait. "Okay, here's what we'll do. I'll head to the liquor store to see if she's there."

Ander stood up. "I'll come with you."

Martin headed toward the door. "Me too."

Now it was Stella's turn to intercept Martin. "No. You take everyone else back to your place. She might be back soon if she's not back already. If she's there, great. We'll continue this party there. With the addition of something white with alcohol and a cork."

Martin gave her a small smile, and the team filed through the apartment door behind him.

As Stella locked the door, a twist in her gut told her she wasn't going to be drinking any wine tonight.

3

A black metal grille protected the door of the Blue Label Liquor Store. Behind the bars, a torn and faded poster advertising a popular brand of vodka was taped to the window. A deep crease cut through the photo, but the advertisement was big enough to hide the store's contents from anyone trying to sneak a peek at the shelves.

Stella rattled the handle. Sharp, metallic *chkchkchks* sounded as the door shimmied in the frame, refusing to open.

A man's muffled voice called through the door. "We're closed. Go away."

Ander reached over Stella's shoulder. He banged on the door, shaking the grille. "This is the FBI. Open up."

There was silence for a moment. Then the voice returned. "FBI? What the hell do you want? Show your badge. I ain't opening the door to no one without no badge."

Stella pulled the badge out of her pocket and slammed it against the door.

She couldn't blame him for being cautious. There was no

neighborhood in the U.S. where a liquor store clerk should open the door after hours.

Two stubby fingers curled around the edges of the poster on the door and pulled it back. A bearded face peered through the gap between the paper and the doorframe.

A bolt drew back at the top of the door, another at the bottom. The lock clicked twice, and a dead bolt clattered back before the clerk opened the door just wide enough to frame his bearded cheeks.

Stella pushed her ID back into her pocket. "What's your name, sir?"

The clerk frowned, pulling a bush of curly black hair into the middle of his forehead. "Randy McDougal. I'm the shift manager here. Also, the clerk, the cashier, the closer, and the locker upper. I do everything except own this damn place. What the hell does the FBI want here?"

Ander lifted his phone and brought up the picture of Jane Lin that Martin had shared. The photo had arrived with a message stating Jane still wasn't home, and her phone was still turned off.

"Have you seen this woman?"

Randy opened the door a little wider. He squinted at the screen and sucked on his lips. The bottom of his face disappeared into his beard.

"Oh, yeah. I remember her. Came in for some Riesling, like we're some kind of fancy California wine store. I told her we got what we got, and if she gots a complaint...well, hell, we may be cheap, but that doesn't strike me as a federal case."

Stella smiled. "We're not here for a complaint. Did you notice anything unusual when she was here? Anything in her behavior that struck you as out of the ordinary?"

Randy scratched at his beard, pondering. "Out of the ordinary? She had a kinda funny accent. New York or something. Probably explains why she went for the Riesling. Most people come in here, they just want some Jack Straight Rye. Got crates of that stuff and no one ever complains."

"How long was she here?"

Randy shrugged. "I didn't count or nothing. Couldn't have been more than five minutes or so. Came in, found some wine, huffed and puffed a bit. Asked me about a Riesling, then left with her Pinot Grigio."

"You remember her buying a Pinot Grigio?" Stella raised her eyebrows, surprised Randy had such a memory for detail.

"I mean, yeah. It was my last bottle. Must've been about forty-five minutes ago. Something like that, anyhow."

Ander rested a shoulder against the doorframe, then immediately stood straight and brushed the sleeve of his shirt. "You got a security camera in there?"

Randy let the door fall closer to closed. "Uh-huh."

"Mind if we take a look?"

"Aw, man. I'm just locking up. I should've been out of here five minutes ago already."

Stella put her hand on the door, partly to stop Randy from closing it on them and partly to lean in, offering a friendly yet concerned smile. "Randy, this is important. You'll be doing us a real favor here."

Randy sighed. He eyed the pair of them, finally landing on Stella's face, then pulled the door open farther. "Come on, then."

Stella followed him into the store. For a moment, she wondered whether all three of them would fit. Randy was her height but had to be two hundred pounds. Though about thirty pounds of that looked like beard and hair. Ander was fit and muscular, but at six foot four, no one had ever called him small.

This store was built for people like Stella—people who were compact and knew exactly what they wanted.

Randy squeezed behind the counter and lifted a small monitor from the shelf behind him. He set the screen in front of Stella and Ander.

The video showed Randy sitting at the counter, his phone in his hand. It took Stella a second to realize the video wasn't paused. The clock on the counter moved from eight forty-five to eight forty-six. Other than the clock ticking, the only thing that moved was Randy's thumb.

Ander nodded to the monitor. "Think you can speed that up?"

"Yeah, just a sec."

Randy tapped a few keys on his keyboard. Still, the only movement on the screen was Randy's thumb. It ran up and down his phone, faster this time, as though he were counting bank notes instead of scrolling social media posts.

"Nine, no. Nine fifteen, no...nine thirty. Here we are."

On the monitor, the door opened. A woman came in. The camera was placed in the wrong corner, so it was impossible to see the customers' faces. She had straight black hair that ended in a neat cut just above her shoulder.

Stella watched the sleek hair as the customer headed to the end of the store and stood before the wine shelves. A short-sleeved navy blouse was tucked into neat, high-waisted jeans. Somehow, though, the woman managed to appear sharp and fashionable in her "mom jeans."

The customer stood in front of the shelves for a few moments. She called something back to Randy, allowing Stella to see her face. She was definitely Martin's sister. Stella could even make out the dimples on her wide cheeks and her thin, arching eyebrows.

Jane Lin placed the bottle on the counter, tried paying

with her phone, and when that didn't work, counted out cash from her wallet.

No purse.

Randy dropped the bottle into a paper bag.

Jane left at nine thirty-eight p.m.

Randy screwed his earbuds back into his ears.

Nothing on the video suggested nefarious deeds. No one seemed to be following Jane or waiting outside...that they could see. Randy seemed barely aware of his surroundings. He showed no interest in Jane Lin or her purchase. It was a miracle he'd even remembered what Jane bought.

There had to be something somewhere, though. People didn't just vanish.

Stella pointed toward the door. "You have the tape for the camera outside as well?"

Ander turned toward the door, surprised. "There's a camera outside?"

"Um, yeah. About an inch over your head."

Ander had the grace to look a little sheepish. "Hey, there're bottles of bourbon in the window. I got distracted."

The liquor store clerk nodded. "Yeah, we got another camera. Right above the door. You got sharp eyes, you." Randy offered Stella a small salute, then typed some things onto the computer.

Stella pointed at the corner of the monitor, at the time stamp. "Start at nine thirty."

The screen changed, revealing the outside of the store. Most of the monitor was dark, but Stella could just make out the sidewalk stretching down the street. The screen sat at a strange angle, making the stretch of cement and street seem elongated. A small puddle of light lit the ground beneath the bourbon-laced window and followed the sidewalk into darkness.

"This is good," Stella said. "The fisheye lens lets us see at least twenty yards in both directions."

Jane crossed into the light, coming from the direction of Martin's apartment. Her feet appeared first, followed by the rest of her body, until she stopped in front of the liquor store door.

Martin's sister opened the door and stepped inside. For the next few minutes, as she chose her wine and complained about the poor selection, nothing happened outdoors.

A gust of wind made an empty cigarette packet roll into the gutter. Moths bashed themselves against the window where light leaked between the grille bars.

Eventually, the door opened again. Jane came out, a brown paper bag in hand.

She headed back in the direction from which she'd come. Then, at the edge of the pool of light, Jane stopped. Stella could only see her from the calves down.

Jane Lin stood there for a moment before turning around and stepping closer to the alley beside the liquor store. She held the wine bottle like a club. Her mouth opened and closed several times, and even though the footage offered no sound, Stella thought the young woman was saying, "Hello?"

A few moments later, Jane disappeared into the alley.

Though they watched for nearly twenty more minutes, fast-forwarding through the footage, she didn't come back out.

Randy stopped the recording.

Stella blew out a long breath. It was always chilling to watch a person in the moments before their death. Stella hoped like hell this wasn't what she was witnessing.

"She clearly heard something and went to investigate." She looked at Randy. "Did you hear something? See anything?"

Randy pointed to the earbuds still lodged in his ears. "Uh-uh."

She ground her teeth in frustration. "You didn't notice anything? No noise from the street?"

Randy shook his head. "Sorry. I was watching a video on my phone. Didn't hear a thing."

Stella pushed herself away from the counter.

"Okay, thanks. You've been a big help. We'll need a copy." She pointed to the camera. The lens focused on the back of her neck. "Move that over behind the register, will you? We need to see faces, not backs."

Randy scratched his beard. "Yes, ma'am."

Stella headed to the door, sensing Ander following her. "Guess we investigate an alley."

4

Martin Lin's apartment was exactly as Hagen had expected it to be.

A beat-up New York license plate hung on the wall above the light-blue sofa. A bookcase contained a few photography books filled with pictures of Manhattan, U.S. national parks, and the world's tallest mountains. But mostly the shelves were loaded with framed pictures of Martin free-falling from a plane, paragliding off a hilltop, clinging to a rope on the side of a mountain, or grinning under his helmet behind the wheel of a stock car.

In the corner of the room, the top half of a globe stood open, offering bottles of tequila, vodka, rum, and more tequila. A heavy wooden coffee table took up most of the space between the sofa, the oversized armchair, and the television and was covered with half-drunk cups of coffee.

The whole team was going to be twitching all night.

Jane wasn't back.

Supervisory Special Agent Paul Slade was on his way.

The situation was real now.

"Does your sister know anyone in the city?" Hagen stood

in the middle of Martin's living room, calling toward the kitchen.

Martin emerged with a plate and a packet of chocolate chip cookies. He opened the packet and poured the contents onto the dish. Hagen wanted the man to sit down and stop playing host.

"No, no one. The only person Jane knows in this town is me. Well, and Caleb and his girlfriend, Sienna. They've video chatted several times."

Caleb wrapped a big hand around his mug of coffee. "Sienna hasn't heard anything. I asked her."

Mac waved her phone as she approached the table and helped herself to a cookie. "And I've still got nothing. Her phone pinged off a tower near the liquor store, but that's the same tower covering your apartment, too, so that doesn't necessarily mean anything. We haven't had a ping since that call, which is possibly more significant."

"You're not getting live data, though, are you? There's a delay, right?" Chloe rested her elbows on her knees. She'd picked the armchair as soon as they'd come in, her small frame almost disappearing into the overstuffed cushions.

Mac nodded. "Right. But the guys in the cyber unit owe me one. They promised as soon as the phone comes online, they'll let me know. I told them Slade will back me up if they get in trouble."

Chloe rocked the armchair. The springs beneath her squeaked. She took over the questioning from Hagen. "How was your sister's mood? This evening, when she left. Is she down here because the stress is getting to her in New York? Is there any reason she'd harm herself?"

"She was fine. Same as always. If you think she might have done something to herself, you're on the wrong track. She's never been like that." Martin threw himself down onto the sofa.

Hagen gave him a small, sympathetic nod. For a moment, he tried to imagine himself in Martin's shoes, waiting for news about one of his sisters, Brianna and Amanda.

The thought caused an ache in his stomach like he'd just been kicked by one of Amanda's horses. He pushed the thought out of his head as quickly as he'd let it sneak in. "What *is* she like?"

Martin held a cookie he'd broken in half in both hands and slowly crushed them between his fingers. Crumbs rained onto the carpet.

"Jane is…you know how Muhammad Ali called some people walnuts? Hard on the outside but soft on the inside? That's her." He bit into another cookie. "She don't take crap from no one. Someone whistles at her in the street, she yells right back so loud their ears almost fall off. But she sees a stray kitten, she'll take it right home and hand-feed that thing until it's all fit and good again. Nothing scares her."

"Nothing?" Hagen prompted, hoping to keep the agent talking.

Martin swallowed and closed his eyes for a moment. "There was one time, she was coming home from work, walking down Union Turnpike, when suddenly everyone starts bookin' it, screaming and running like Godzilla was chewing up buildings or something. Some crazy was on a rampage with a knife. Well, Jane dodged past the crazy and ran straight to one of the victims and kept pressure on that wound until the ambulance arrived. Saved the woman's life."

Caleb patted his friend's shoulder. "If someone's taken your sister, man, they've bitten off more than they can chew."

A knock sounded twice on the door.

"That'll be Slade." Chloe left the armchair, which continued rocking and squeaking after she'd stood.

But when she opened the door, the person waiting on the doorstep wasn't the tall, graying figure of the team's boss.

It was a young woman with long light-brown hair highlighted with tasteful blond streaks. She wore a blue pantsuit that was far too expensive for Martin's apartment and held a Dior clutch in her manicured hands.

She peered past Chloe into the living room. "Is this Martin Lin's apartment?"

5

As they stepped into the alleyway, a sharp mixture of urine overlaid with rotten vegetables and a bitter scent of vomit assailed them. Stella held her nose. "Okay, so she entered here after seeing or hearing something."

"Maybe the smell punched her in the gut."

Stella pulled her phone out of her pocket and turned on the flashlight. There was nothing to suggest anything odd or out of place. No spots of blood. No torn bits of clothing.

The phone's beam landed on the corner of a rusty dumpster. The smell was stronger here, a thick odor of sweat and unwashed clothes adding to the urine. Stella drew closer, running the beam over the top of the dumpster. The light revealed piles of overstuffed garbage bags tossed on top of the lid, some torn and spilling their contents over the edge.

She sighed. "We've got to look."

Holding her breath, she slipped between the dumpster and the wall. Something, perhaps an old head of lettuce, fell from one of the empty bags and burst at her feet.

Ander lit up his phone. "Want me to go first?"

Stella rolled her eyes. "Might have asked me that before I got halfway in."

"Just waiting for the right moment."

She moved farther in, stepping sideways to avoid touching the wall or the dumpster. The circle of light cast by her phone reached another pile of garbage bags on the other side. "Really, a formal complaint to the disposal company wouldn't be out of bounds here. This garbage has been sitting here for a while."

One of the garbage bags rustled.

Stella froze.

The bag froze.

The rustle returned.

Stella bent her knees, bracing herself. One hand moved toward the pistol on her hip. She licked dry lips.

"Ander—"

Meeow.

A cat leapt from the bags, bounced over the top of the dumpster, and disappeared into the night.

"What the hell?" Ander's voice sounded loud and high.

Stella stood straight, letting her own heebie-jeebies go. "Didn't scare you, did it?"

"Me? No. Well, maybe a little. It was a panther, right? We can say it was a panther."

Stella removed her hand from the back of her holster and placed it on the wall for balance. The bricks were damp and slippery. She yanked her hand back, wiping it on the back of her pants. "Ugh. Gross."

She'd reached the end of the dumpster, and she advanced deeper into the alley. Behind her, Ander shuffled closer.

Chicken.

Normally, it would be the fastidious Hagen behaving so delicately.

Stella pointed the light from her phone onto the ground.

She didn't know—and didn't particularly want to know—why the concrete here was damp. The white LED beam lit small black puddles of *something* on the ground.

A coil of aluminum shaving had somehow sprung out of another trash bag.

And there was a pair of dirty sneakers, their soles torn, their laces long gone.

And the pair of legs to which they were attached.

Stella froze. She moved the light farther up, taking in patched cargo pants, a dirty t-shirt with a neckline stretched halfway down a thin, scabby chest. Her eyes rose upward to a messy gray beard and the gapped teeth of the man grinning up at her.

The man lifted a hand to shield his eyes from the light. "Hey, lady. Put that thing away. Ruining my night vision, is what you're doing."

Stella lowered the light. The man dropped his hand but quickly raised it again, bringing a brown paper bag to his lips. He sucked on the bottle inside thirstily.

She pulled out her badge. "FBI Special Agent Stella Knox. What's your name, sir?"

"My name? Ain't no one used my name for a loo-oong time. Skeg's what people call me now."

"Did you see a young woman come this way recently, Skeg?"

Skeg grinned again and scratched at his beard. The motion made a loud rasping sound on a face that clearly hadn't been washed in weeks.

"Just got here, lady. Good place to sleep, right here. Nice and quiet. Ain't no one come down this alley, not even in the daytime. Nice and out of the way."

Ander was finally at Stella's side. He must have slipped down the alley as soon as he heard Skeg's voice. He shined his light on the man's face, prompting him to turn his head.

"Hey!"

Ander ignored Skeg's protest. "Out of the way and close to the liquor store. That's convenient."

Skeg raised the bottle in a *cheers* gesture. "Didn't even need to go in there tonight. Found this whole bottle just lying right here. I'm telling you, man, this alley's better than one of them fancy hotels. 'Cept they don't put a chocolate on your pillow. I got a whole bottle of…" he pulled down the bag and squinted at the label, "Pinot Grigio. Don't get that at the motels I stay at." He chuckled a wet, watery laugh.

Stella grabbed the bottle, the bag crackling under her fingers.

Skeg scrabbled to take it back, his swipe missing by a couple of feet and about three seconds. "Hey, that's mine! You go get your own."

Stella pulled the bottle out of the bag. Only about half the wine remained. The label described the bottle's contents as dry and white. Stella peered into the bottom of the bag and removed a small square of paper.

The receipt declared that the bottle came from the Blue Label Liquor store and was time-stamped at nine thirty-seven that evening.

"Skeg, this is very important." She knelt closer to the man. A wave of body odor and garbage can and smoke crashed into her. Stella gritted her teeth against the smell. "Where *exactly* was this bottle?"

He pointed to the dumpster. "It was right next to the dumpster. There."

"When did you get here?"

Skeg stared at her as if she had two heads. "I don't got a clock on me. Maybe ten?"

Stella began connecting the dots. Jane Lin had left the liquor store at nine thirty-eight p.m., according to the footage, with this bottle of Pinot Grigio. The store closed at ten thirty, which was when she and Ander arrived. Skeg found this bottle somewhere between those two times. Based on how he'd made himself at home among the garbage bags and by the amount of wine he'd consumed, Stella thought Skeg's ten p.m. estimate was correct.

All of this meant Jane had come into this alley, and *something* had happened.

Something bad.

She looked at Ander.

His phone was already at his ear. "I'm calling Slade now."

6

I dropped the broken chair. It clattered to the ground, one dented leg leaving a quarter-sized smudge of blood on the floor.

She lay there and groaned, still begging me to stop, even though I had stopped moments before. There was new blood on her temple, and her lip looked split. I took a deep breath and held it, trying to maintain a sense of calm. It wouldn't do to lose control again.

I pointed the flashlight on my phone at the stage. "Get back up there. Go on. Get moving."

She crawled, struggling to move over the mess on the floor. Construction—or rather, deconstruction—detritus littered the floor. Her head hung low as she slithered along, as though straightening would hurt too much. When she reached the edge of the stage, I grabbed her upper arm and pulled her up.

"Back there. All the way to the end. You move again, woman, I'll beat your brains out. God help me, I will."

She tried to stand up, but her left leg gave way, and she dropped again to the stage floor. I pushed her. She fell onto her side and crawled until she reached the back wall and curled into the fetal position.

For the first time since I'd caught her trying to escape, my inner intensity settled down. The sight of her at the door infuriated me, and I lost my mind a bit. Grabbing the nearest object, I'd wailed on her with a chair leg.

The bruising and cuts along her back would be extra wounds for my FBI friends. Her brother would feel every one of those injuries. He would understand my pain.

Oh, yes. They would all understand.

I picked up my bag.

The weight of the axe inside was heavier than I'd expected, solid and reassuring.

I climbed onto the stage after her. She lay there, whimpering, but I ignored her. The room itself interested me more now.

So many memories were packed into this building.

Outside this room was Hell itself. The lockers were long gone—casualties of extreme vandalism—but I'd never forget the smell of the dog shit I'd find inside mine with *Freak* and *Weirdo* scrawled on the door. So many times, I'd been shoved cheek-first into their steel walls.

The other classrooms lined the corridor outside. They should've been places that made me feel good, a safe space to chat with classmates and laugh at shared jokes. Yet I'd sat alone in the corner while everyone chatted among themselves.

And at the end of the day, I'd return to a house that was so often empty.

This room, though, *this* room was the only place I could escape. The piano used to stand on the corner of that stage. As soon as I pulled in the stool and put my feet on the pedals, everything else faded away. Nothing but the melody and rhythm remained.

That was all I needed.

I turned toward the wall where the FBI agent's sister lay on her side. Fresh blood made a trail from the back of her head, past her ear and down the side of her neck.

Once I'd realized what music could do, I knew I had my escape. My headphones never left my ears after that. As soon as class ended, I'd slip them on and let Bach or Beethoven, Chopin or Tchaikovsky penetrate my ears and echo through my head. I needed nothing else.

All the time I'd attended this school, I'd been alone. Except at home, where I lived with my father. Now he was gone too. All that remained was music—and a burning, rising urge to make them pay.

7

From his vantage point in the middle of the living room, Hagen took in the woman at Martin's door. She wasn't quite a blond or brunette, but somewhere in between. Her eyes were an amber shade that somehow seemed to be the exact same color as her hair. Attractive, in a simple, tidy kind of way. Elegant.

She extended her well-manicured hand toward Chloe. Her fingers were pressed together, and her arm was straight. The stranger's posture was ridiculously formal, as though she were introducing herself at an embassy garden party instead of gate-crashing the ruins of an end-of-case party.

Chloe looked down at the woman's hand, then back up at her face. "Who the hell are you?"

Hagen narrowed his eyes. Under normal circumstances, he might have found Chloe's aggressive greeting over the top. Tonight, however, wasn't a normal circumstance. Martin had just received a threatening phone call from a voice that sounded vaguely female, and now there was a strange woman on his doorstep.

One hand drifted toward the grip of his pistol.

Beside him, the muscles on Caleb's neck tensed. Martin looked set to leap off the edge of the sofa.

If this was the woman who'd called on Jane's phone, Hagen doubted he'd be able to stop Martin. Or that he'd even want to try.

Chloe continued to ignore the woman's outstretched hand. "Gotta tell you, lady, if you're here to sell life insurance, you're talking to the wrong people."

The woman lowered her arm. "You must be Chloe Foster." Her voice was short and clipped, but somehow friendly. "Semi-pro kickboxer. Recently wounded in the line of duty during the capture of the Curator Killer. I'm glad to see you appear to be one hundred percent again."

Chloe looked confused, but she didn't move from the door. "Says who?"

The visitor didn't answer. She turned her attention to the agents in the living room. Her gaze landed on Hagen first. "You must be Special Agent Hagen Yates. This is your seventh posting in four years. You were recently in the news for resolving the situation in Kentwood, shooting Boris Kerne, the hostage taker, and rescuing four hostages."

Now Hagen's hand did grasp the grip of his pistol. He said nothing, his jaw set. This woman had clearly done her homework on the team. It was unsettling.

The visitor took in each agent, one by one, but didn't seem inclined to step through the door without an invitation. Her ability to read the room appeared spot-on.

"You must be Special Agent Caleb Hudson, specializing in white-collar crime and organized crime methodologies. Special Agent Mackenzie Drake, cybercrime fighter extraordinaire. And you…" She paused, her lips drawn into a thin, sympathetic line that appeared to be genuine. "You must be Special Agent Martin Lin."

Chloe took a step forward, blocking the visitor from

entering the apartment. Hagen had never seen her kick a woman in the face, but he was fairly certain he would be seeing it in a moment.

"I won't ask you again, lady. Who the hell are you?"

The visitor straightened her back. If Chloe's threat frightened her, she didn't show it.

"I'm Special Agent Stacy Lark. I'm filling in for Danielle Jameson while she's on maternity leave." She gripped her clutch with both hands. "I expected to meet you all in the office tomorrow, but SSA Slade asked me to meet him here." She raised to her tiptoes and looked over Chloe's shoulder. Since Stacy was about four inches taller than Chloe, she didn't have to strain too hard. "I don't see him. Is he…has he arrived?"

Hagen released the grip on his weapon as the pieces fell into place. Stacy's appearance and demeanor read as an overachieving brainiac rather than a violent maniac.

"No. He hasn't." Chloe still didn't move. She wasn't the trusting type.

Hagen moved toward the door. "Chloe, stand down. You can let her in."

Behind Stacy, an elevator pinged. A moment later, Slade's deep voice penetrated the room. "Yes, Chloe, you can let your new colleague in."

Chloe, keeping her sharp blue eyes on the new team member, pulled open the door and stood to one side.

Stacy stepped into Martin's living room. Slade followed, brushing by Chloe. His phone was pressed to his ear, but he lowered it as he made straight for Martin, resting a hand on his shoulder.

"How are you holding up?"

Martin swallowed hard. "Not great. She's been gone too long. We gotta find her, Boss. We gotta get her."

Slade's nostrils flared. "Don't worry. We'll find her."

Chloe moved to the sofa Martin was sitting on. "This could all be nothing, you know. She could walk in here any minute, saying she's been walking around for the last hour, looking for her lost phone."

Martin pushed to his feet. "You're wrong." He looked around the room, at all his colleagues. "What are we all doing *sitting* here? We need to be out there right now—"

"We *got* people out there." Caleb's deep voice was calming. "Good people. Your job is to sit here and wait. Hardest job in the damn world, but you got this."

Slade put both hands on Martin's shoulders this time. One of the things Hagen admired about his boss was his ability to remain calm in the midst of big emotions. "No one is going to be sitting. I just got a call from Ander. They think they've got something. Looks like Jane went into an alley near the liquor store. We don't know why, but the bottle of wine she purchased was found by the dumpster there. There was no sign of her or her phone."

Chloe frowned. "What would she go into an alley for?"

Hagen rested his elbows on his knees. "That's what we've got to find out."

"Right," Slade agreed.

Martin shifted from Slade's grip and reached for the keys on the small table by the door. "I'm going down there."

Slade grasped Martin's elbow and steered him to the sofa, not letting go until Martin was seated.

"No. You're going to wait right here. We do this together. Like always. Your job is to stay here with Caleb in case she calls or turns up. I also need you to call the Nashville police. We don't have jurisdiction right now because we don't know for certain if this is a kidnapping. Besides, we need more eyes on the street. Mac, Chloe, go to the office and see if you can dig up anything on area traffic cameras. Hagen, you stay here. I'll take Stacy and meet Stella and Ander on site."

8

Stella lifted a garbage bag with her one good hand and dropped it behind her in the alley. The bags towered over her, climbing the wall like poison ivy. "I'm pretty sure someone needs to be fined. You can't just *leave* trash for this long."

The amount of stuff to sift through was almost unending.

Stella adjusted her latex gloves, wishing she had stronger, needle-resistant ones, and reached for another bag. She'd found nothing so far. No sign of a struggle, of scattered drops of blood or torn clothing. Only the half-empty bottle of wine and its receipt indicated Jane had been here.

And poor Skeg, who wasn't pleased about losing his prize.

He stood outside the alley, arguing with Ander, his slurred words drifting over the top of the dumpster.

"Hey, man, that's my bottle. I found it fair and square. You go get your own."

Ander held the bottle away from him. "It's ours now. This is evidence. And I'm sure you want to assist this investigation as much as you can."

"Evidence, huh? So is there, like, a reward or something?

There should be a reward for helping the FBI. What do I get, huh?"

"You get the thanks of a grateful United States."

"That's it? Aw, c'mon, man. You should at least get me another bottle. Least the United States could do, seeing as it stole mine."

Ander sighed and called back into the alley. "Hey, Stella. What do you say you let me dig through everything, and you take this guy to get another bottle?"

Stella dragged another garbage bag down. The sacks were light enough to lift with her uninjured hand, but her busted rib shot electric bursts across her torso. Still, digging through trash sounded better than spending more time with Skeg.

"Store's closed." She hopped out of the way as something spilled and pooled on the asphalt next to her.

She'd asked Ander to get Skeg out of the alley while she trawled through the garbage. Mostly, she didn't want to admit her injury was limiting, despite the sharp pain in her side and the ache in her arm. She wasn't going to let Boris Kerne's bullet hold her back—not in some stinking, garbage-laden alley.

"Sorry, Skeg. You'll just have to do without your nightcap. How are you doing in there, Stella? Found anything?"

Stella stepped back and scanned the bags. Nothing stood out.

"Nope. I don't know if we'll find anything here. Not in this light and working by ourselves. I don't even know if there's anything here to find."

A headlight beam burst through the darkness, flooding the alley as an SUV pulled up on the street outside.

Stella held up a hand to protect her eyes from the sudden glare.

Slade stepped out from the driver's seat, and a tall, slim woman left the passenger side. They strode over. "Ander

Bennett, meet Stacy Lark. She's filling in while Dani's on leave. Stacy, that's Stella Knox down there. Moving garbage by the looks of it. Found anything, Stella?"

Stella waved her latex-covered hand in greeting. Something dripped from the end of her fingers. She hoped no one noticed.

"Nice to meet you, Stacy. I'm not usually neck-deep in garbage."

Stacy wrinkled her nose. "It's a job hazard."

Stella answered Slade's previous question. "I've found nothing so far. Ander's holding our one clue."

Ander pulled the bottle out of reach as Skeg swung for it again and missed. "And this is Skeg."

"*My* bottle of wine. Damn thieves, is what you are."

Slade frowned. "That'll do. Who are you, Mr. Skeg?"

Skeg drew his back straight. He tottered sideways and tried again. "No mister necessary. I'm Skeg. And that's my bottle. I dunno who you people think you are, but you can't go round stealing stuff from honest citizens."

Slade pulled out his wallet and removed a twenty-dollar bill. "This is for the bottle. What you do with it is up to you, but I'd recommend spending it on a hot meal or a change of clothes instead of a couple of bottles of this cheap crap."

"What keeps me warm is my business." Skeg reached to grab the twenty.

Slade pulled the money away. "What did you see?"

Skeg scowled. "I told your friends here. I didn't see nothing. The bottle was just sitting there when I came here to bed down for the night. Just had to shove the cork inside and I was all set for a good evening. 'Til y'all showed up and ruined my plans."

Slade nodded and handed Skeg the money.

Skeg snatched the twenty and tottered away from the alley.

"Hey," Ander called after him. "Where can we find you if we need you?"

Skeg shrugged and walked on. "I don't go too far. You're standing in my damn bedroom. And bathroom."

Stella cringed as she dragged another bag out of the way. "What's happening at the apartment?"

"There's been no contact. Mac says the phone still hasn't come back online. Chloe's found nothing on traffic cameras. The nearest camera is about five blocks away and there's plenty of small streets that run past it."

Stacy coughed. Even in the dim light on the street, Stella could see she was holding a hand under her nose to block the smell.

Stella smiled. She was already used to the stink and barely noticed it anymore.

Still, the new agent moved forward. "I...I don't see any forensics."

"No." Slade scratched his chin. "This is not official. We're just helping a friend here."

Stella reached for another bag, the last in the first row of garbage bags before she had to start working her way higher up the trash mountain.

As she pulled the sack away, something caught her eye. On the ground, just hidden by the corner of the bag, was a lever about twelve inches long with an angled head and a ridged hole.

The tool looked like it should have been used for removing bolts or wheel nuts, but the head was too small for a tire iron. Its thick wooden handle was too clean and shiny to belong in that alley, where everything was covered in damp, rotting garbage. The end of the tool, on the other hand, was darkly stained. Stella recognized blood when she saw it.

Near it, the cement was splattered, almost in perfect

circles, indicating blood had dripped straight down off the gadget. A tiny smear, like something—a foot or a pant hem—had been dragged through some of the spots.

Stella lifted a hand. "Think I got something." She flipped her phone over, turning on the camera feature. A few preliminary shots recorded how she'd found the spots. She also took a few shots of the tool—the shiny handle and the bloodstained metal end. "Get me an evidence bag."

Holding the tool between a latex-covered finger and thumb, she left the alley and joined Ander and Slade. Stacy pulled out a clear bag from the rear of Slade's SUV. She held it open as Stella dropped the strange tool inside.

"What have you got?" Slade used the headlight gleam to examine the item, stopping at the stained end. "Okay, that could be blood."

"There's some blood spots on the ground, too, I think." Stella leaned in, closer to Stacy.

All three of her colleagues took a step back. Stella wanted to laugh. She must've stunk like a demon. Ander lifted a finger to his nose.

Stella rolled her eyes. "If you think *you* smell any sweeter, Ander, I've got news for you."

"You were down there a lot longer than I was." He held the evidence bag out in front of him, turning the tool first one way, then the other. "I've got HemaTrace in the car. We can find out if it's blood for sure." He paused, frowning. "What the hell is this thing, anyway? Looks like something you'd use to tighten the bolt on Frankenstein's neck."

Stacy, apparently more used to their terrible smells now, leaned in. "Frankenstein was the inventor, not the monster. That's a piano tuning hammer."

Stella, Ander, and Slade stared at her.

Her cheeks reddened. "My mother plays the piano."

Stella lifted her eyebrows. "Another pianist, huh?"

"Me? No. I learned the cello instead. It was my act of rebellion."

"You rebel, you. Actually, I was talking about our last case. That one involved a pianist."

"Oh, yes. Of course. Boris Kerne, a professional musician with an awful lot of grudges. Those poor people. Shot. Garroted. Sounded like a truly terrible series of crimes. Paul told me all about it."

Paul? Did people really call Slade by his first name?

"Yeah, his playing wasn't all that *noteworthy* either. Very slow."

Ander grinned at Stella's pun, took the potential weapon to his car, and grabbed the HemaTrace testing kit from the trunk storage pocket.

Stella watched while he took a sample of the blood and dropped it into the testing vial to let it do its magic.

"Thirty minutes and we'll know whether this dark spot is human."

Slade nodded, acknowledging the update. He turned to Stella. "All right. Anything else that's relevant?"

"I'm not sure. It had to have happened fast. The door to the liquor store is here." Stella walked to the Blue Label's front door before pointing up. "There's a camera there, and we saw her walk about this far." She took a few steps forward, making it a couple yards before stopping. "Then it looked like she hesitated for some reason. The video's rough. We could only see from the knees down as she walked out of view. But maybe she heard something? Then headed into the alleyway. It wouldn't be hard to stage an ambush."

"It's certainly dark enough," Stacy agreed. "So you think it was a blitz? Someone surprised her?"

"That's my best guess. Maybe he used the piano tuner or maybe something else in there." Stella waved a hand at the alley, meeting Slade and Stacy at the entrance. "We'd need a forensic team to go through all that. It's a job and a half. And we don't even know if we've got a crime yet."

"No. You're right. We don't. All right, look, there's nothing else we can do at the moment. I'll get a BOLO out and make sure Martin filled out a missing persons report. I'll have Caleb stay with him. For now, go home and get some rest. Hopefully, this will all turn out to be nothing. I want everyone in the office at eight sharp tomorrow morning unless we hear something in the meantime."

"Um, Boss?" Ander called from behind his car. Everyone turned to him. He held up the plastic results rectangle. "We have human blood."

9

Jane Lin hugged her knees to her chest, curled onto her side. If only she had the strength to sit up, to kneel, to push herself off the floor. She'd bust through the door and try to run until she found someone who could help. Surely, there had to be someone in the area who could call the police and stop this crazy person.

Her abductor sat at the end of the stage, one leg hanging over the edge, a canvas backpack at their side. For half an hour, they hadn't spoken or moved. Whoever it was just hummed a tune Jane almost recognized.

Humming, humming, humming.

Jane's vision blurred. She saw double and couldn't focus. As hard as she tried, Jane couldn't tell if the hooded figure was a man or a woman. Even the sound of the humming wasn't high-pitched or low.

When Jane had tried to speak through her pain, to ask what this person wanted or plead to be let go, the kidnapper hadn't moved. The biggest response Jane had received was a quiet shush and pieces of that hummed melody.

The room was too dark. Thin lines of gray light still

shone through the high windows, cutting a fuzzy border across the stage, but not enough to help her. Jane lay on one side of the light, her abductor on the other. All Jane saw was the hummer's shifting silhouette, a black pair of shapes in a black room.

Jane thought of all her convicted clients. There were only a handful—she was a very good defense attorney. Most were still in prison, and she was sure this person wasn't among the parolees. There was nothing familiar about the figure at the edge of the stage.

And besides, she was so far from New York. No one would have followed her all the way down here. Would they? Her decision to visit Martin had been almost spontaneous, the result of too many canceled plans.

Martin.

Her brother should have been here. He must be putting the entire apparatus of the FBI to use to find her. Jane was sure he'd succeed.

He has to.

Somewhere high outside, an owl hooted.

"Stupid bird. Put me off my tune."

Jane barely heard the hummer's voice through the steady buzz going through her ears. She needed medical attention. The pounding in her head was escalating, and she worried that her vision and hearing would never recover from tonight.

With all the strength she possessed, Jane pushed herself back across the floor. She had nowhere to go, and every move made her head and neck ache worse, but the more distance she could put between this person and herself, the better she felt.

Despite the pain and her inability to focus, Jane decided to try conversation. She was always good at getting clients to open up. Often, she provided the safe space they needed to confess. The brain fog was heavy, though. Words were difficult.

"Who...who are you?"

"*Who-who?*" The laugh that trailed the mocking was as neutral in tone as the humming. "Now you're the one who sounds like an owl. Like the great Lewis Carroll wrote, *The owl got the dish as his share of the treat*, you know. *When the pie was all finished, the owl, as a boon, was kindly permitted to pocket the spoon.*"

A chill passed through Jane. That was nonsensical. Lost in their own world. Insane. She couldn't reason with someone like that. But she had to try. She had no choice. But something had gone wrong, not only between her brain and her ears and her brain and her eyes, but also her brain and her mouth. "If...money...can...arrangement. Not rich. But...can help."

The humming shadow rose to their feet.

Jane saw two sets of black boots, and she blinked, but her double vision remained. If her head wasn't thumping and the bruises on her arms and back didn't already ache, Jane might have fancied her chances in a fight. The hummer wasn't large.

Sure, she hadn't hit anyone since Kate Broad in the sixth grade, but she felt like throwing a punch right now.

Jane pushed herself into a sitting position. The whole room shifted. But she tried to stand, pressing her hand into the back wall for balance. She only made it halfway up before a wave of nausea hit the back of her throat. She slipped back down to the floor of the stage.

The kidnapper lifted the bag and drew nearer. "I don't want money. There's just one thing I want, and it's something you can't buy."

The hummer laid the bag on the stage and opened the

zipper. The *zzzz* sound buzzed in Jane's ears, adding a different layer to the tinnitus. It sounded like bees.

"What...you want?"

"I want...revenge."

When the hummer stood straight again, the double beams of light from the window glinted against the dual edge of a small axe.

Jane closed her eyes as another wave of nausea hit her.

She couldn't escape the laughter, though, or the words that followed.

"Off with her head!"

10

Hagen sipped his espresso, hoping the caffeine would kick in right away. He'd expected Friday to be pretty quiet, mostly paperwork. But after the late night and with no word about Jane this morning, he needed to focus.

With the last case so recently solved, he'd expected today to be easy, a chance to catch up on paperwork before heading down to Atlanta with Stella the following morning.

For much of the last case, getting back to Atlanta had dominated his plans. He wanted nothing more than to drive south, knock on Joel Ramirez's door, and demand information about his father's killer. Joel Ramirez or Matthew Johnson—or whatever the hell his name was—had known everything about Memphis's drug rings. The man must know something. Anything.

And yet, here he was, back in the office conference room at eight in the damn morning. The lack of news about Jane Lin twisted Hagen's gut, telling him something was wrong.

Very wrong.

He couldn't leave Martin alone. No one could.

Stella sat opposite him, sandwiched between Chloe and

the new girl, Stacy Lark. Ander took the seat next to him. Mac was at the end of the table, trying to will the small computer in her hand to give her answers.

Answers were out there, Hagen was sure. But they weren't coming through on Mac's phone.

Slade closed the door gently behind him before addressing the room. "As I'm sure you all know, there's no news. Jane still hasn't come home and there's been no message."

Mac held up her traitorous, uncooperative phone. "Her phone hasn't come on again either. The last ping was still from the liquor store area around nine forty. That was when Martin received the phone call."

Slade sat at the table, steepling his fingers as he always did when trying to keep everyone calm and collected. "I realize this is worrisome for Martin, and I realize you were all there when he received that troubling call. The local PD and highway patrol is alerted and on the lookout. They've agreed to keep us in the loop."

The knowledge wasn't a great comfort, but Hagen felt a bit better knowing there were multiple eyes on the situation.

"And it's important to remember Jane Lin is a grown woman, and it's only been a few hours. It's still possible, even probable, that she'll walk in at any minute having...I don't know, drank too much in a bar and slept it off in the park or something."

One glance around the room told Hagen no one was buying Slade's last bit of reassurance. Jane Lin was a successful New York lawyer. She wouldn't have gotten drunk in a strange town without someone with her, like Martin.

Stacy leaned toward Stella. She whispered, but the room was small enough for Hagen to hear. "Is Martin's sister known for drinking too much?"

New girl is sharp.

Stella shook her head. "She's not known to us at all. This is her first time down here. It's possible she's playing a joke on him. Martin can be a bit of a joker. But—"

Chloe dropped a fist onto the table. "But if she is, I'll kill both of them myself." She leaned forward, staring Slade in the eye. "You're right, Boss. It hasn't been long. But if an agent's relative goes missing like this, I'm going to assume we've got a problem."

Ander nodded. "The HemaTrace test on the piano tuning thing came back positive. We rushed it to the lab for more testing. We're waiting for a Rapid DNA result. They swabbed Martin to test for any biological match."

Hagen swallowed the last of the espresso and folded over the lip of the cup. Ander had sent them pictures of the unfamiliar tool last night. It reminded Hagen of a fancy socket wrench. The piece had a solid hardwood handle with a metal rod extending out, ending in a star-shaped socket.

He'd seen Martin's face when Caleb broke the news about the positive preliminary blood test. Martin's tan face turned pale, and he collapsed onto his sofa, his head in his hands. He was convinced the test meant something had happened to his sister.

In all honesty, Hagen was too.

But the tool could've come from anywhere, at any time. It'd been found among piles of garbage. None of that meant it was involved in Jane's disappearance.

Trying to convince a family member not to worry—yet—was next to impossible. Hagen knew from experience.

He tossed the cup into the wastepaper basket and watched it bounce off the rim before landing with a satisfying thud. "What is that thing, anyway? Exactly?"

Stacy answered. "A piano tuning hammer is a special kind of wrench used to tighten piano strings. You use the wrench part to turn the tuning pins under the lid. I've seen my mother use her piano tuner on our baby grand at home."

Hagen raised his eyebrows. *Her mother's piano tuner? My family didn't have a piano tuner. A piano, yes, but not a tuner.*

"And it can draw blood?"

Stacy inclined her head slightly, sending her blond-brown hair cascading past her shoulder. She seemed to be making a calculation in her mind, dividing the thickness of a scalp by the weight of a piano tuning hammer multiplied by the momentum of a violent swing.

Just when Hagen was certain she'd fallen asleep, her head popped up. "I suppose it could. The one Stella found was quite a solid thing, with a good heavy counterweight on the end. I suspect that if you hit someone on the head with such a tool, you might well draw blood, yes. Especially if you were to hit them repeatedly."

The room fell silent.

Only a few days ago, Hagen had watched a pianist rise from behind a keyboard, level a gun, and fire. And that was after the killer had shot four people and garroted three others with piano wire.

Were all musicians mad?

Stella seemed to be thinking along the same lines. "Maybe there's a link to the last case?"

Hagen shook his head, more to convince himself than Stella. They shouldn't allow previous cases to color present cases. "Boris Kerne is dead, remember? I put three bullets into him. I don't think he's plugged his holes, escaped from the morgue, and picked up his piano tuner."

She shot him a *ha ha, very funny* look. "I'm not saying that. But we've got a link to pianos in two consecutive cases. What are the odds?"

Stacy responded before Hagen could answer. "When I was in the Philadelphia police department, we found two men dead in the space of three weeks. *Both* were clutching guitar cases."

Ander lifted an eyebrow. "And?"

"And the cases weren't connected at all. The police cases, that is. Not the guitar cases. Although the guitar cases weren't connected either. They just belonged to two victims who both happened to play the guitar."

Hagen stared at her for a moment. He blinked. Then he turned to Stella. "For all we know, a piano professional might've thrown the tuner out after he cut his finger on it. Maybe a local business owner dumped it with all the trash. Or maybe some homeless guys got in a fight and grabbed the closest trash at hand. We don't know if the blood is hers or if the piano tuner has anything to do with anything."

A buzz sounded at the head of the table. Slade reached into his pocket and pulled out his phone. He took the call, holding up a finger for quiet. "Slade."

For a moment, his face was expressionless. Then the color drained from his cheeks. His eyes closed, and he slowly lowered the phone from his ear.

"Boss?" Stella's voice was quiet as a whisper.

"She's dead."

11

Stella knew what it was like to lose a sibling.

The room spun around her head. The walls seemed to shift, one corner chasing another until all direction was lost and nothing made sense.

She remembered the numbness that followed the loss of her brother, the loneliness that had filled her over the following weeks and months. Losing Jackson meant no one would ever understand her or share in her experiences or laugh at her childhood stories the same way he had.

Since cancer had taken her brother, there had always been a part of her that was missing, forever dark, forever alone.

Martin would know that feeling, too, now.

Hagen appeared to have deflated. The back of his neck rested against the top of his chair. His arms hung loosely at his sides, and he seemed to be examining, though with closed eyes, the surface of the ceiling.

Ander's face was hidden behind the palms of his hands.

Stacy's gaze passed from one person to the next, uncertain of where to focus. Stella understood. The new agent was a stranger and wouldn't know how to read them yet.

Mac's head was in her arms.

Chloe beat her fist against the top of the table, vibrating the whole length of it. Her lips moved, but Stella could only hear screaming in her own ears, as constant and unending as the sea smashing onto the shoreline.

Slade tapped the top of the table with the knuckle of his index finger. "Okay. With me now. That was Caleb. The Nashville police are at Martin's apartment. Caleb will stay with him. I'll head over there as soon as we're done here."

Hagen opened his eyes. His face was stony, but she knew there was a rage, deep and hot, behind that expression. When he spoke, his voice was too even, too controlled. "What happened?"

Slade folded his hands together and rested his arms on the table. Stella noticed his knuckles were white. Hagen wasn't the only one holding in some strong emotions. "Surveyors found her body in the basement of a derelict school just outside the city. The building was scheduled to be demolished. A wallet was found in the victim's back pocket with Jane Lin's ID."

Mac's face was almost as white as her hair. When she spoke, her voice was tight. She was clearly holding back tears. "Will…will Martin have to go and make an ID?"

Slade shook his head. "I doubt it. I expect we'll use fingerprints and dental records for this one."

A coldness swept through Stella. "Why? What happened?"

If Martin wasn't allowed to make the identification, there had to be a reason.

And that reason wasn't going to be good.

Slade lowered his chin. "The victim was decapitated."

Stella took a deep breath and released it. It didn't help. Slade's words had settled on her chest, heavy like a bowling ball, and a few slow, deep breaths weren't going to alleviate the pressure.

Hagen's countenance had somehow become even stonier, even harder.

Slade stretched his neck to the side, his spine popping at the movement. "There's more. It appears the killer left a message for us. There was writing on the wall. '*Chop, chop, FBI.*'"

Hagen nodded, something in his jaw relaxing. "This is one for us, then."

Stella watched Hagen closely. He wanted to go after the murderer. He wanted this case. He wanted revenge for Martin's loss. After his questionable choices during the Boris Kerne case—ignoring her instructions right before the confrontation, firing at the suspect, and acting rashly—she needed to keep an eye on him.

"It is." Slade lifted his head. His jaw was set, and a fire lit behind his eyes. "So let's get to work. Chloe, Ander, I want you two back in Martin's neighborhood. Check out every business that might have a camera aimed at the street between Martin's apartment and Blue Label Liquor Store. If there's something on tape, I want it."

Chloe shot him a salute. "Yes, sir."

"Mac, Stacy, you two stay here and trawl the records. I want to know if there's anyone in our team's case history…a recent parolee, another victim, or someone who beat the charges…who might be a fit for revenge killings. And follow up on that piano tuner. If that *is* Jane Lin's blood, add professional musicians or music-related professions to the criminal record search. Stella, Hagen, you get the crime scene. Get out there. Now."

12

Sis chewed a bite of oatmeal cookie as she rewatched the footage from FBI Special Agent Stella Knox's apartment. What she'd just learned from the bugs and camera she'd planted in the agent's apartment was troubling.

Very troubling.

She dropped a third spoonful of sugar into her coffee and stirred. Her camp chair creaked as she stretched her legs.

The heat of the morning was already starting to rise, but in the shade of her trailer, the weather was still bearable. In front of her, just beyond the double bar fence and through the tree line, the meadow behind the trailer park was coming to life. The grass, browning now in the early summer, waved in the breeze and sent out a rich scent of damp earth and burnt straw.

One day, when all this was over, she'd own a place like this. Somewhere far from anyone, accessible only by a single dirt road. Somewhere no one would disturb her. She'd live there with someone special. There'd be just the two of them and enough money to make sure she'd never need to see anyone or do anything ever again.

Turning back to the footage on her phone, she frowned. Sis could deal with one busybody. Even if they were in law enforcement.

Killing Stella Knox would take some skill, but she had no doubt she could do it. She actually welcomed the challenge.

In addition to Stella, she had her sights set on that friend of hers. Hagen Yates, all square-jawed. A pretty boy with repressed emotions. So cliché. Dealing with him would be easy.

Heck, it would be fun.

But an entire FBI team? The thought knotted her stomach. That was a whole different kettle of fish. No one could take out a whole team. And the tighter the team members were, the harder it would be to pick off even one or two.

Dammit! The Officer was wrong. He should have let me act when I wanted to. Delay just makes everything a thousand times harder.

And she'd have to tell him.

"Damn."

Sis hit the pause button and sipped her coffee.

Then she put down her mug and rubbed her temples. However pleasant the view might have been, and however welcome the coffee and cookies were, the thought of calling The Officer left a sour taste in her mouth.

That would not be a pleasant conversation. And right now, she just wanted something pleasant.

Just do it.

Thumb hovering over her phone screen, she took a deep breath but tapped a different number instead.

"Hey, sweet cheeks. Was just thinking 'boutcha."

Sis smiled and settled into her chair. This was so much better.

His voice was always so comforting. It made her feel safe and confident. She hadn't seen him for almost a month.

While she'd managed to push him out of her mind for much of that time, hearing his voice reminded her of what she missed.

She just wanted to be home again and in his arms.

"Oh, yeah? What were you thinking about?"

"Ha. Wouldn't you like to know."

"Yeah, I'd like to know." She lowered her voice a few registers, lacing it with sex. She slipped down into the chair. "Go on, you can tell me."

He chuckled. "I was just thinking…"

"Yes?"

"I was just thinking…I had to make my own damn coffee this morning. I'm telling you, Sam, I'll be hella glad when this job's over, and you're back here."

Sis pushed herself up. She was back outside her trailer, wishing she were somewhere else. "Yeah, me too. Glad to hear you've missed my coffee, at least."

He had a warm laugh with just a hint of edge, as though his mood could change at any moment. It made the sound more welcome, more valuable.

"Yeah, I've missed ya, sweet cheeks. And not just because the sink is filling up with dirty dishes." He lowered his voice until it was almost a growl. "You *know* what I've missed most."

Sis's stomach clenched, low and deep. "Yeah, me too. Believe me. Me too."

"Ha, so what's up? How's it all going up there?"

She sighed, not wanting to talk about business. "Not great. Heard some stuff on the recording last night that's gonna make my life a thousand times harder than it needs to be. She's told everyone, the entire team. They're all working together. And now I'm gonna have to call The Officer and let him know. I'm telling you, I should have just…done what I wanted to do at the beginning."

"Shh!" His hiss was hard and angry. "You know better than to talk like that on the phone."

Sis rolled her eyes. She was a professional. There was nothing incriminating in their conversation...unless he started pointing things out. "I just meant I should have taken her out for coffee, that's all."

"Yeah, okay. Hey, listen. You want my advice?"

"Sure. Just don't mansplain while you're offering it."

He didn't laugh like she thought he would. In fact, he didn't say anything for the space of at least twenty heartbeats.

When she worried the call had dropped, he finally spoke. "You keep your mouth shut."

That wasn't what she expected. "Excuse me?"

"That's what you need to do. You keep your mouth shut and don't tell The Officer a damn thing. He won't thank you for news like this. He'll just blame you, and you know how that'll turn out."

Sis reached for another cookie and took a big bite. She *did* know how things would turn out if he blamed her.

The Officer had blamed her brother and ordered her to take care of the situation. She'd taken care of the situation, all right. She'd killed her brother and taken over his position.

Using the excuse of chewing to give herself time to think, she finally swallowed. "But I'm going to have to tell him eventually. Better now than when things are worse."

"Who says things are gonna get worse? Just because they're all working together doesn't mean they're going to get anything done. We could be looking at too many cooks in the kitchen right now." He blew out a breath.

She heard him shuffling around. He always paced when he got agitated.

"I know what I'm doing."

"Listen, all I'm saying is hold off a little. Just 'til you see how things are panning out. There's no point in putting your neck on the line if you don't need to."

Sis was in no rush to speak to The Officer, but if Stella's team made progress, she'd have to let him know soon. "All right. But I won't be able to keep this from him for long. A day. Maybe two, tops."

"That's good enough. What's Stella—"

"Shhh...no names."

"Right. So what's No Name's team up to now?"

Sis dunked the remaining half of her cookie in her coffee. The soggy edge broke away, leaving small pieces to float in her cup.

"They're busy. Again. One of their sisters went missing." She licked the coffee off the cookie but didn't take a bite. This was too exciting. "It's a lucky break. They're off-balance. If we wanted to make a date, this would be the time."

"Just be smart, okay? They're gonna be off-balance for a while. Don't tell The Officer any more than he needs to know and watch them closely. Here, I'm going to text you something you're gonna just love."

When her phone pinged, she lowered it and looked at the screen.

She smiled.

Hagen Yates's home address.

13

Stella trod carefully down the Merys High School stairs, avoiding bits of wood and plaster. Graffiti covered most of the walls with illegible tags and obscene images. Behind her, Hagen swore quietly as the bottom of his shoe slid on a piece of timber.

When she reached the basement level, there were several specialized classrooms. A choir space with disassembled risers to her left, followed by a band room with metal music stands bunched together. On her right was the rehearsal room—the crime scene.

She squeezed through the half-open door and froze.

The air was thick and coppery. A sharp stink of drying blood—a lot of it—combined with dust and mold that had been left to grow far too long. She stood in the doorway and coughed, trying to catch her breath.

Hagen waited behind her, acting as though the heaviness in the air didn't bother him at all.

The basement room was dim. Only a thin line of broken windows high on the far walls let in any direct light. A forest of broken chairs littered the floor, their legs sticking up like broken saplings. In the spaces between their bent branches, pieces of plaster and shattered glass stuck out.

A stage dominated the front of the space.

Two crime scene officers, anonymous in identical white Tyvek suits, worked the area.

At the back of the stage, next to the wall, lay a human torso. Blood covered the top of the woman's short-sleeved navy blouse and stained her jeans. One sneaker still clung to the woman's left foot. The other stood in the middle of the stage, as though waiting for a spotlight.

Above the body, words were scrawled in thick white chalk. *Chop, chop, FBI.*

Stella held up her ID and addressed the two officers at the scene. "Stella Knox and Hagen Yates, FBI." She paused and lowered her voice. "Where's the head?"

One of the officers pointed to the far corner of the stage. "Over there. Grab yourself a couple of suits and come take a look. I don't think she'll mind if you stare."

Stella wasn't in the mood for their prototypical dark humor. Not on this case.

A cardboard box rested by the doorway. She pulled out two suits, handed one to Hagen, and climbed into the other. She closed the Velcro and pulled the covers over her shoes as best she could with her left arm in a cast.

The other crime scene officer approached, sidestepping the debris.

"FBI Special Agent Stella Knox, huh? Should have known I'd find you in a place like this."

Standing in front of her, framed by the white hood of his forensic suit, was the square face of Dan Garcia, her last partner in the Nashville PD. Little more than half a year had passed since she'd left the department, passed through training at Quantico, and been assigned to the FBI's Nashville office.

He hadn't changed at all. Dan's salt-and-pepper mustache was still neatly trimmed. His dark eyes still sparkled with unshared jokes.

The unchanged nature of his appearance threw her for a moment. She seemed to have lived at least half a dozen lives in the same amount of time. Stella wondered if she still looked the same.

"Dan, fancy seeing you here."

"Yeah, real fancy. A derelict building and a body in two parts. You know, if you wanted to meet up again, Nashville has some pretty good bars with much better atmosphere." He put his gloved hands on his hips and raised his eyebrows. "But that would hardly be Stella Knox's way, would it?"

She forced a smile.

Their last case had ended with two men dead in a suburban house and Dan hit in the ribs by a ricochet.

Now *she* was the one with a rib busted by a ricochet.

"Nah, what's time with Dan Garcia if it doesn't involve at least one dead body and one broken rib?"

Eyeing the hand on her side and the cast on her wrist, he frowned. "You okay?"

"Remnants from the last case. Nothing serious."

He shook his head. "Stella Knox. Always getting into trouble."

Hagen stepped past her into the basement, the hood of his Tyvek suit pulled up over his head.

Dan eyed him for a second. "You her partner?"

Hagen nodded. "You bet."

"You need to take better care of her. Looks like she's been through a war."

"Usually, she's the one who has to look after me. If she hadn't given me a hard shove on the last case, I'd be the one with the sore side and possibly a lot worse." Hagen stepped past them and approached the stage.

"That right?" Dan watched Hagen from the corner of his eye.

The Nashville officer had been one of Stella's mentors. He'd been patrolling the streets for fifteen years, and he'd taught her plenty. But she'd seen more murders over the last few weeks than he'd seen in his entire career.

"So where's the head, Dan?"

Her former partner pointed to the far corner of the stage and called to the other white-suited officer. "Over there. Hey, Mags! Want to show Special Agents Knox and...what was your name?"

Hagen tugged on his latex gloves. "Yates. Special Agent Hagen Yates."

"And Special Agent Yates. You want to show them the rest of the body?" Dan leaned toward Stella. "Maggie Edwards is our new assistant medical examiner. Thought we'd break her in nice and easy. With a basement decapitation."

Maggie dropped an evidence bag into a box. "Come on up." The newbie assistant M.E. was short and heavily built, with blond eyebrows just visible under the line of her white hood. If an early career encounter with a two-part corpse bothered her, she showed no signs of concern. "This way."

Stella and Hagen navigated the mess of broken chairs toward the stage. She glanced back to spot Dan watching them, his hands on his hips. Maybe he'd done enough close-up investigating for the moment.

"You know, Stella, nice as it is to see you again, we can handle a murder without you. We've been doing okay since you left."

Ignoring Dan, Stella heaved herself onto the stage.

Up close, the body looked particularly forlorn.

Jane Lin was on her side. Her head had been cut off, and not cleanly. Stella could count three or four separate strokes based on the ragged wound. Blood had poured out over the stage like a dam breaking.

The head had rolled to the corner, blood splattered across her face, her dark eyes—so like Martin's—were open. Her shoulder-length hair stuck to her cheeks and clumped where it rested in her coagulated blood.

Stella swallowed. "Jeez."

Dan climbed up onto the stage behind her. "Yeah. We can even handle a killing as messy as this by ourselves. And we were, until we got a call telling us to back off because the FBI will be coming in to do our work for us."

Hagen approached Jane's head and crouched in front of it. He spoke without turning. "She's the sister of one of our guys. This is personal."

Stella nodded toward the chalked message. "And probably a direct threat to us."

She faced the assistant medical examiner. "What can you tell us?"

Maggie stepped toward the back of the stage, avoiding the puddle of blood that had flooded from Jane's neck.

On the wall at the back, three tall lines of blood spatter rose up the peeling paint like the spray from a small hose, the height of the jets receding from right to left.

Maggie crouched in front of the corpse and pointed a rubber-clad finger at Jane's neck.

"The head wasn't removed with the first blow. She was able to crawl a little before she died. Look here. Do you see how there appear to be different cut marks on the neck?"

"Yes." Stella squatted next to Maggie. Beneath the stump were two slightly darker lines where blood had soaked and settled.

Maggie pointed higher up on Jane's head. "There's another cut on the head. My guess is that the kill wasn't clean." That confirmed what Stella had noted earlier. "She probably took three or four blows with a sharp instrument, each while she was still alive. That's why those blood sprays move across the wall."

Stella stood, her shoulder bumping Hagen's chest. She hadn't noticed him leaning over her. He stepped back, giving her space. She took the opportunity to put some distance between herself and the remains and to push down the queasiness roiling her stomach.

It was strange. Hagen hated examining bodies in morgues. He appeared much more comfortable on scene, no matter how gruesome.

"Are we dealing with a killer who's not particularly strong?" Stella asked.

Maggie unrolled a black body bag. "Maybe. But even professional executioners have been known to struggle to remove a head. Mary Queen of Scots needed three blows to lose hers. And the poor Countess of Salisbury, Margaret Pole, took ten or so whacks with an executioner's axe. Your victim here might have been lucky."

Stella made her way to the door, pulling down her hood and tugging the Velcro straps of her suit. "So you think the murder weapon was an axe?"

Maggie pulled out an identification tag and wrote on the label with a sharpie. "I really couldn't say at this stage."

Dan helped unzip the body bag, holding the flaps open for Maggie. "We didn't find a murder weapon. You find it, you let us know."

Hagen joined Stella at the door. He looked relieved to remove his suit. "What's the story with this place, anyway?"

"This place?" Dan rocked on his heels. "Merys High School's been derelict for a few years. Been set for demolition. Pretty open, though. No security. Anyone can come in, as you can see from the graffiti on the walls. Body could have been here for a while if a couple of surveyors hadn't come in this morning. Looks like the new owners are trying to make progress."

Stella peeled off her gloves. Usually, the removal of the latex and the return of fresh air on her skin made her hands feel clean and free again. But now, she wanted to keep her hands behind her back and not touch anything. Just being in the basement, with its darkness and its dust, its body and pool of dried blood, made her feel dirty.

"What about footprints? There's enough dust here to leave plenty of marks. The newest ones will be marked by the least dust."

Dan grinned. "I'm sure forensics will be all over that. I'll let you know if they find anything."

"Thanks, Dan."

Stella squeezed through the half-open door but stopped to look back at the stage. The headless body was almost unrecognizable as a person. It could have been a mannequin or a large doll, something entirely inhuman.

Whoever Jane Lin had been, whatever she had thought, felt, or dreamed about, was gone.

Stella's brother had fared better, but not by much. In his last days, he had been so thin and frail, barely a shadow of the fit, young man he was before his illness.

Death is a merciless thing.

14

I was lost.

The music swept me away. Brahms's first piano concerto, one of the first pieces I'd ever played and still one of my favorites. The gentleness of its opening before the rise in tempo in the *adagio*, that sudden burst of energy and speed that—

My finger slipped. Instead of pressing cleanly on F-natural, the tip of my finger also landed on the edge of F-sharp.

Ridiculous. Insane.

I didn't move. The sound continued, that dissonant chord.

Somewhere deep in my guts, frustration and anger bubbled.

How could I have misplayed? How on earth could I have got this wrong?

I knew this piece by heart. I'd played it since I was a child. If I chopped my fingers off and laid them on the keyboard, they'd play that piece by themselves.

Really. The number of times I've played this piece without ever making a mistake...

I took a deep breath and started again with the *maestoso*. There was that harmony, those repeated chords. They were all so familiar, like a visit from an old friend, their return as sweet and welcome as morning coffee. There was the small talk in the introduction before the conversation turned to the exciting, juicy gossip we'd both been waiting to discuss.

Oh, Brahms, you sly little thing. You really knew how to talk. No wonder Clara Schumann was so enamored.

I played on. It was all so easy, so comfortable, until...

Clang.

I'd murdered the time. Landed wrong again.

"Dammit. Damn you to hell!"

I slammed the keyboard closed and mashed my fists on the lid. Mistakes. More mistakes. All morning, I'd been making mistakes.

My head. The problem was all in my head. But of course, my head was a mess. I'd lost my father. I'd just gotten him back, and now I'd lost him for a second time. Permanently. No wonder I couldn't think, couldn't hear, couldn't control my own hands.

That was what had happened last night. I'd lost control. My hands moved on their own, without thought or intention. They just moved as though driven by nothing more than instinct and an innate expectation of what I needed to do next.

They just *knew*.

I stared at the back of my hands. My fingers were long, the nails clean and neatly trimmed. These were hands that made music. Their movements sprinkled beauty into the air, removing all stress and worry from entire auditoriums. All those reflections on money and promotions and what the children are going to get up to next. They all disappeared when my fingers started moving along a keyboard. That was the power they contained.

And what had they done last night? It wasn't something beautiful, that was for sure.

I shoved the piano stool away from my legs, grabbed a toy rabbit from the top of the piano and held it close. My fingers buried themselves in its soft, thick fur so that I could see little more than the summits of my knuckles.

For a moment, the rage that burned inside me subsided. The hunger waned, its teeth retracted.

Maybe I shouldn't have done it. If I hadn't seen that FBI agent on television that night, standing in front of the place they'd killed my father and calling his killer a hero, maybe it wouldn't have happened.

It was their fault…again.

I'd have just mourned. Lost myself in music as I always did. The notes were always there for me, and I was sure I could have buried myself in them again and stayed there until the rage passed.

But once I'd seen Martin Lin's name on the screen, music no longer allowed me to escape.

I tracked down his address. He wasn't far from a music store I frequented. I needed a new tuning hammer, and I went to see him after I finished my errand. I didn't know what I was going to say. I might not have said anything at all.

When I reached his building, I found his name on the mailboxes. His apartment was on the third floor of a five-story building in a questionable part of the city. He must have spent all his money on those expensive clothes and fancy shades I saw on television. His rent was probably less than mine.

My hand hovered over the doorbell. I didn't ring it.

My stomach twisted. My hands shook. I didn't know what I'd do if I saw him. Push him down the stairs, perhaps, and watch him bounce and break until he couldn't be put back together. Or maybe

I'd scratch his eyes out like a cat, or...or...oh, I didn't know what I'd do.

Whenever I'd felt that urge to punch someone, to dig my fingers into their skin and pull them apart...when I'd felt that demand growing within me, rising and expanding, I'd always turned to my piano and thumped the keys until sweat ran from my brow and my fingers were sore from the pounding.

That was what I'd always loved about the piano. Whatever you gave it, however much you abused it, the instrument would still be there the next day, ready to be played again.

So I didn't ring the bell. I stood in the shadows on the other side of the road and waited and watched.

A woman arrived. She dragged one of those little trolley suitcases, like some kind of world traveler. She pressed the button that belonged to FBI Special Agent Martin Lin's apartment. I immediately knew she was related to Lin—they looked exactly alike. He must've buzzed her in.

Music flowed through my head then. Tchaikovsky. No one could hear it but me, and I let it play. Every note, every cadence. I listened to them all as though I were in the concert hall, seated right next to the grand piano.

Just as the piece ended, the door opposite opened and Lin himself came out.

The music stopped. The world fell silent. There he was, just walking down the street without a care in the world, like he hadn't just been boasting on television about my father's killing.

He climbed into his car. The engine rumbled, and he was gone.

The street was silent. Tchaikovsky had stopped. The piano was closed, the lid locked. I remained there in the shadow of the doorway opposite and didn't move. I couldn't say what I was waiting for, only that no force on Earth could have made me shift.

The evening drew on. The sun set. The door opened again, and out she came, the woman who'd rung his doorbell.

I followed her, staying on the other side of the road and

avoiding the streetlights. She turned down a dark road and disappeared into a small liquor store.

The plan formed slowly, until eventually, all I knew was this woman meant something to Special Agent Lin and that hurting her would hurt him. That was good enough for me. I wouldn't let the chance slip away.

There was an alley near the store. I hid in the entrance, staying out of the light, and when I saw her come out, I called her toward me.

She stopped. Turned back.

I wasn't sure what to do then. Nothing was planned, but I did have a burning rage tearing through me, such a desire to make that FBI sonofabitch feel some of my pain.

Slipping into the alley, I scrambled under the garbage bags until I was almost entirely buried and gripped the tuning hammer I'd just bought. Thinking ahead, I wiped all the fingerprints off before using a plastic bag as a makeshift glove.

I called again. She came.

So curious. So keen to help.

When she was standing right over me, when she'd taken out her phone and started to call, that was when I swung, nailing her in the back of the head.

Crack.

That blow was such a release, like the second at the end of a crescendo, as though everything I'd thought and felt and done since my father's killing had been building to this moment.

And so, I did it again. And again. The rush just kept getting better.

Minutes passed but they felt like hours, and I didn't move. She lay on the ground, silent, a small line of blood matting her hair while I stood there trembling. Until something clicked, and I knew exactly what I had to do.

I left her there just long enough to bring my car around. When I threw her body in the back seat, everything was just a blur.

My head whirled. I thought she was dead until she groaned. My foot moved by itself, and then my hands. I pressed the gas. A few minutes later, I was pulling up at my old school.

The rehearsal room. That was the best place. No one would hear her there.

And that was when I realized I'd forgotten the tuning hammer. I must have left it in the alley. Such a stupid thing to do.

Didn't matter in the end. I'd wedged the door closed and gone hunting for another tool.

I found something better. Much better.

And I did it.

Wasn't as easy as I thought it was going to be. Was a lot messier than I thought it would be too. But, oh, the relief. Such sweet relief passed through me when I was done. I would never have thought revenge could be so satisfying. Best performance I'd ever had.

I hugged my rabbit tighter and paced from one end of the living room to the other. The fire was rising again. Remembering what I'd done was fanning the flames. The urge to play again was coming.

In front of me, in the middle of the mantelpiece, was a picture. A copy of an illustration of the Queen of Hearts. She'd know what to do. She'd know exactly what to do to someone who'd harmed her father.

I roared as she roared, throwing my arms wide. "*Off with their heads!*"

As my voice died, the head of my toy rabbit was in one hand, the body in the other. Stuffing drifted through the air and settled over the floor like snow.

Glad this bunny wasn't my favorite. I had a drawerful. He hadn't even made the top ten.

"Who's next?"

My eyes went to the copy of *The Tennessean* on the coffee table, the pages open to the story of my father's death. There was a picture of the music store where he'd been murdered, and a man with a square jaw and an FBI jacket. His gun was in his hand.

Special Agent Hagen Yates. The agent who'd shot the suspect. I stared at the picture, fury burning inside me.

"You. You're next."

15

Stella sat on the curb in the shade of an ash tree opposite Merys High School. She rested her elbows on her knees. The day's heat was building, draining her energy. Sweat glued her t-shirt to her back. But the hot, fresh air was preferable to the dust and the humidity and the metallic smell of the blood in the basement behind her.

Somewhere to her left, past their FBI-issued SUV and Dan Garcia's unmarked late model Ford Interceptor sedan, beyond the medical examiner's van and the line of yellow police tape, a wood chipper hummed—then screamed—as it ingested logs and spat out splinters. The noise bored into Stella's head, thumping on the inside of her skull. She put her thumbs to her temples and rubbed.

What the hell are they doing over there?

Hagen sat next to her, stretching his legs into the empty road. "You okay?"

Stella rubbed harder, her thumbs making small circles next to her eyes. "Not really."

"Mm. Not an easy one in there. Gruesome. But I think the dead kids and the cheerleaders were worse."

Dead children were every law enforcement officer's worst nightmare. The team had come across too many of them in the last few weeks. Teenagers poisoned, beaten, shot.

But Hagen was wrong. The sight of Jane Lin's body, hacked and beaten, drilled deeper than their recent young victims had.

Because this time, she'd see the grief.

She'd be with Martin as part of his world broke away, drifted off to never return.

The death of a sibling did that. In the days after her brother's death, Stella hadn't wanted to speak to anyone. She rarely came out of her room, barely exchanged a word with her mother who, she realized now, needed both to comfort and to be comforted. Stella had been too numb to listen, in too much pain to open up.

There was nothing Stella could do about the grief coming to Martin. But he'd also want justice. There *was* something she could do about that.

"We can't let him down, you know. We just can't. We have to find the person who killed his sister. You and me, we know what it's like not to get justice. We can't leave Martin the same way. We have to find whoever did this and bring them in."

"Or find whoever did this and leave someone else to carry them in."

Hagen nodded toward the medical examiner's van. The new Assistant Medical Examiner Maggie Edwards pushed the gurney carrying Jane Lin's body, now contained in a black body bag, toward the open rear doors of the van. "We do our bit. She does hers."

Sometimes, death was the easy route.

Stella shook her head. "If that's what we have to do, we will. But I want to see this bastard in court. I want to see the look in the sonofabitch's eye when the jury returns the verdict and the judge hands down the sentence. I think that's what Martin will want too. Nothing will beat that satisfaction."

Hagen leaned forward, mirroring Stella's position. His dark green eyes were somber. "You're so naïve, Stella. You really think that's what's going to happen? This bastard will just get themselves some lawyer with a sharp suit. That sharp-suited lawyer'll find some technicality and plea the murder down to a misdemeanor that gets our murderer off with time served. If you want justice in this world, you have to do it yourself."

Stella had never heard him speak like this before, so clearly, so dismissive of the justice system he was a part of.

Ice lodged somewhere in her chest. With a deep chill, she saw it all now.

They'd confront Joel Ramirez.

Her dad's former partner would give them a name—an old crime boss or a crooked cop or a gang leader.

And instead of opening a case, instead of carefully gathering evidence and bringing the criminal in, Hagen would take him somewhere dark and quiet and leave the body for a medical examiner to pick up and push into a drawer at the morgue.

"You can't mean that."

A muscle in Hagen's jaw twitched. "Damn right, I do. How many times have you picked someone up only to see them walk out of the courtroom a free person? A hundred? A thousand? We can go inside and ask your friend, Dan, if you want. He looks like he's been around. I'm sure he's got story after story about picking up some scumbag, shoving him through that revolving courthouse door, only to have the scumbag come right back out. Again and again. Jeez, Stella, there's a reason my dad had a roster of regular clients."

Stella had to make him see that wasn't true. "So everything we do, everyone we arrest, you think it's all for nothing? You think Cecil Meester will see daylight again? Or Darwin Rhodell? Those guys are going to spend the rest of their lives making license plates and looking at the sky through barred windows. And it's thanks to us."

Hagen put his head in his hands and sighed. "Sometimes the system works okay. Other times you've got to prepare to get your hands dirty and do it yourself."

Goose bumps raised on her arms.

"We're not judge, jury, and executioner. We're investigators. The system isn't perfect. *Nothing's* perfect. But we've got to trust the courts. They work better than you believe, and you'll find that out firsthand if you take the law into your own hands. Because the courthouse door they'll shove *you* through won't spit you back out again anytime soon."

"I don't care." Hagen's words sounded like they'd come from a dark, sad, faraway place. "Even if someone was to catch me, which I doubt, and even if a jury of my peers convicted me for taking vengeance on some big-time lowlife, which I doubt even more, I don't care. Nothing else matters. Don't you get that? Nothing matters but finding the sonofabitch who murdered my father."

"And you think you can do that? You think you have the *right* to do that?"

"I do. And I need you and your help to find him. I'm not asking for anything else. The rest I can do myself."

As his words echoed inside Stella's mind, neither spoke.

The wood chipper screamed as it tore apart another log.

Hagen sat straight and brushed the sidewalk dust from his palms.

"At least...that's what I used to think. Seeing everyone when you asked for help? The way they all came together, how they were willing to help you, even though this isn't their fight." He picked a small stone out of the heel of his hand. "It was a pretty good reminder of what a team can do."

"Try to remember that, okay?"

He flicked the stone into the road. It bounced and stopped under the wheel of the SUV. "You know I'm taking a big risk telling you this, right? You asked me once if I trusted you. Well, this is how much I trust you."

Stella pulled her knees into her chest. Yes, she'd asked if he trusted her, but this wasn't what she meant. She wanted to know if she could count on him—if he had her back when she needed it.

Seeking vengeance compromised him. Such powerful emotions meant Hagen might lose focus, which was dangerous. If push came to shove, would he honestly help her, or would he make an emotional decision, endangering her and the team?

Not that she didn't understand the desire. Of course she did. She, too, felt that desperate, burning need to find the person who took her father away.

She wanted to tear him limb from limb, to scatter his parts and rid the world of him.

Anger and rage, they were natural emotions. They came from the heart. She could understand them. But those emotions, and the actions resulting from them, often made things worse.

Justice? That was the head talking, and the head could talk louder than the heart if you were just willing to stand back and listen to it.

Stella placed her hand on Hagen's arm. She gripped tightly. "Thank you for trusting me. But Hagen, you *cannot* do this. Forget what that scumbag *deserves*. You know what vengeance does. You know how it corrupts, how it turns the person who follows it into a monster. You can't go that way. You're no monster."

Hagen looked down at Stella's hand. "Maybe you're right. I promise not to do anything reckless. Okay?"

Stella released his arm. He sounded sincere, but she didn't quite believe him. She needed another pair of eyes on him, a sharper pair than hers, with a stronger arm.

She smiled, but the effort didn't last. "Listen, what you said just now about teamwork? You're right. We can do more together. So I'm going to bring in Slade."

His eyes widened. "Wait. You can't do that."

Watch me.

"Yeah, I can. We have to. I'm going to—"

"There you two are." Dan Garcia crossed the street to join them. "Taking a break, huh? Not like you, Stella."

Dan stood over her, his eyes hidden behind his sunglasses, his mouth a straight line under his mustache. The sun was directly behind his shoulder. Stella had to squint as she peered up. She pushed to her feet, wiping the palm of her good hand on the side of her pants.

"It's a meeting, Dan. Lots of meetings in the FBI."

"Is that right? Can't say you're making me jealous there. Just wanted to tell you, I found some footprints. Debris in the basement and the blood on the stage mucked everything up, but I found a good, clean set off the side of the stage. Still waiting for the forensics guys to turn up, but they'll take a copy and see what they can find."

Hagen stood and rested his lower back against the side of the SUV. "What did the prints look like? Anything you can tell us about them?"

Dan peeled off his sunglasses. "Can't tell you much about the prints other than the size looks small…smaller than the victim's. Looks like a boot print. But since it's so small, I imagine we might actually be looking for a woman."

That was a surprise. "A woman? Really? And you're sure it came from our killer?"

"No, I'm not sure, but I can't rule it out. It's the print with the least amount of new dust, which you so wisely said to search for." A van pulled up by the side of the road. Dan lifted a hand in greeting. "That'll be forensics. Late as always." He moved off to greet the forensic team. "I'll let you know what they find."

Hagen reached for the door handle of the SUV. "What do you say? Back to base?"

The screech of the wood chipper wailed again.

Stella shook her head. "No, not yet. Let's see what's going on with that wood chipper."

"Really?"

Images of the gruesome scene inside the old school were replaced by others. "Ever seen *Fargo*?"

16

Stella crossed the road and followed the grinding screech of the wood chipper.

At the end of the street, where the curb faded into broken stones and dusty earth, a house stood, set back from the road. The building was a single story, its wooden siding shingles bent and faded. The gutter had detached itself from part of the roof, and the front yard was overgrown. In the corner of the yard, a woman fed logs into a small wood chipper.

Stella put the woman's age somewhere in her sixties. She wore a thin summer dress that once might've been a light blue but had long faded into a dull gray. Her white hair was pulled into an untidy bun. Scratches and bruises covered her bare arms. Tall black boots protected her feet.

She didn't look up as Stella and Hagen approached. Instead, she bent and grabbed another log from a pile next to her. She called out without looking up from her chore.

"You people here from the law?"

Stella stopped short of where wood chips shot out of a hole in the chip bag. "Yes, ma'am. I'm FBI Special Agent Stella Knox. This is Special Agent Hagen Yates."

The wood chipper screamed again.

Stella saw that Hagen hung back a little, eyeing the small copse at the edge of the property, looking for boot tracks on the dry ground.

The woman scratched the side of her head with as much energy as the machine in front of her crunched the wood.

Stella waited for the machine to stop.

The woman still scratched.

"What's your name, ma'am?"

"What's that?" The woman pulled out a foam earplug and pushed her ear closer to Stella. "Hearing's not what it used to be. You'll have to speak up."

"Your name, ma'am," Stella yelled. "What's your name?"

"Anne. Anne Lawson. You come about the thieves?"

What the hell? "Thieves?"

Anne cupped a hand to her ear. "Leaves?"

"Thieves!"

"That's right. Thieves. They steal my stuff. Steal my logs. Steal my wood chips. Steal my tools. Steal my bottles."

She waved an arm toward her house. Stella made out at least half a dozen wine bottles, twice that number of beer bottles, and several square bourbon bottles on the porch beside the front door.

Hagen rocked on his heels, impressed. "Do you live here alone, Anne?"

Anne cupped her hand to her ear. "What's that?"

"I said, do you live here alone?"

"Yep, just me. S'all I need now. Don't need no more. No more husband. Ran off with some Asian chick. Welcome to him. Good riddance. That's what I say."

She put her earplug back in, threw another log into the chipper, and stood back. The bag at the end of the machine shook and swelled. Wood dust drifted over the front yard.

Stella wondered whether Mrs. Anne Lawson held a

grudge against "Asian chicks." She waited for the noise to subside to no more than a low rumble. "Were you here last night, Mrs. Lawson?"

"Sure was. Where else would I be? Got nowhere to go."

"And did you see or hear anything unusual?"

"Did I what? You gotta speak up. Can't hear too good no more."

"I asked if you heard or saw anything unusual last night."

"Last night? No, nothing strange. Heard an owl, but that's not strange. Didn't notice nothing else. But had an early night, if you know what I mean. Just me and ole Jack Daniel's." She laughed, scratching the side of her head and disturbing a thick lock of dirty gray hair.

Hagen pointed at the pile of logs behind Anne. "You chop those yourself?"

Anne shrugged. "When you ain't got a man, what you gonna do?"

"Where's your axe?"

Anne picked up a log and weighed it in her hand before dropping it into the chipper. "Where's my what? My axe? That's a good question, that is. Was kinda hopin' you were here to tell me that."

Hagen scratched his nose. "Sorry, but no. Do you know where your axe is?"

She turned in a circle, peering in all directions. "Must have left it lying around here somewhere. Got a habit of losing things. Sometimes, I think little folks from the woods come in here and take my stuff and move it behind the sofa and such." She chuckled. "Why? You offering to do some chopping for me, Mr. Agent?"

She grinned again, a bigger smile that revealed a mouth full of stained, gapped teeth.

Hagen offered a somewhat insincere smile. "I'd love to

help. And I'm sure my colleague would too. But we're kind of busy."

"Ain't we all." Anne tossed another log into the chipper. "Ain't we all."

After the screech of wood finished, Stella stepped forward more aggressively. "Turn this off for a second, Mrs. Lawson. This is important."

Anne Lawson arched her eyebrows. "You think what I'm doing *isn't* important?"

"Turn it off."

Anne stopped the machine and crossed her narrow, scratched-up arms across her chest. "What's so important?"

"We're investigating a murder that's happened in this neighborhood. I need to know exactly what you did last night, who you did it with, and I need you to explain your injuries." Stella glanced pointedly at Anne's arms.

The older woman spat on the ground in front of her. Stella imagined the wood grit was permanently lodged in the woman's gums. "Last night, I watched television by myself, but I called my mother at around ten. She's in a home and doesn't know what time it is most of the time. Had a nightcap and went to bed."

"And your arms?"

Anne held them out so Stella and Hagen could see the injuries up close. Some were fresh, others healing. "I get cut all the time. You think this machine is cute and cuddly?"

"Thank you, Mrs. Lawson. You've been a big help." Stella reached into her pocket and pulled out a card. "You give me a call if you remember anything, okay?"

Anne took the card and scrutinized it carefully, as though the phone number beneath Stella's name was the combination to a Swiss safe-deposit box.

"Uh-huh. Sure thing."

Stella headed back to the SUV. Behind her, the motor of

the wood chipper whirred to life. As she opened the passenger door, she stopped and looked over her shoulder. Anne threw another log into the chipper and then tossed Stella's card in after it.

"What do you think?"

Hagen leaned on the roof of the car. "I think she has a lot of empties. From what I gather, she and Skeg would make a cute couple."

"She does. Which means she makes a lot of trips to liquor stores. Think those scratches could be from Jane Lin defending herself?"

"Send a message to our new assistant M.E. and make sure she gets fingernail scrapings from Jane." Hagen slipped into the driver's seat. "I don't think she chopped those logs with the side of her hand either. I think we need to check out ole Anne Lawson."

17

As Hagen took his seat in the meeting room at the FBI's Nashville Resident Agency, he envied Dan Garcia.

Stella's former partner, now a detective, was probably still at the crime scene, supervising forensic officers and ensuring that no curious passersby or nosy reporters trod all over the scene.

It wasn't the most enjoyable of jobs, but it was better than sitting in a conference room.

Ander sat next to him, saying nothing as he spun a pen around his thumb like a drummer. When Hagen asked about it once, Ander told him he'd picked up the twirling habit from Martin right after the New Yorker arrived at the Agency. Still, he only did it occasionally, when he was lost in thought or had recently been spending time with Martin.

Sitting there, Hagen could see exactly what Ander was thinking and who he was thinking of.

Mac came in with Stella, Chloe, and Stacy Lark.

Stacy took the seat next to Stella, leaving Mac the chair at the end of the table. Mac frowned at the back of the new girl's head. Mac normally sat beside Stella.

Before she could protest, however, the door opened again, and Slade entered with Caleb.

Mac was the first to speak as she took her seat. "How's Martin doing?"

Slade didn't sit. He rested his fingers on the back of his chair and let Caleb squeeze past him. "Not great."

Caleb sat and ran a hand over the top of his closely shaved head. "I just brought him in to pick up some stuff he left at his desk. Maybe a different environment will help." Caleb sighed, which seemed to deflate the big-framed man. "He and Jane were close. He's blaming himself now. Thinks if he'd been there with her, none of this would have happened."

Slade gave Caleb a solid, single pat on the shoulder. "Which is why we've got to find whoever's responsible for this and do it fast. I've managed to get this case put on our docket. It's in our zone, and the message makes it one for us. But I've had to swear that we could do this professionally and dispassionately as part of a joint task force with the local police department. Don't let me down."

The conference room door opened.

Martin stood in the doorway, and Hagen was immediately concerned by his appearance. His face was pale. Dark rings circled his eyes. His hair, which was usually neatly combed and gelled, stood up in a thick clump at the back of his head. The last button on his shirt was undone, and a flap hung over the belt of his pants.

"You're talking about Jane's case."

Slade shifted toward the door, clearly trying to head his bereaved team member off. "We're in the middle of a meeting. You're officially on compassionate leave. Why don't you go wait at your desk? Caleb can take you home in a few minutes."

Martin strode past Slade and perched on the corner of the table. He crossed his arms over his narrow chest. "Uh-uh.

If this is about Jane, I want to listen. You carry on. I'll stay right here. I won't say a word."

Slade gripped Martin's upper arm. "You can't be here."

Martin stared at Slade's hand. He didn't move. "You got a suspect yet?"

Slade pulled gently but firmly. "Martin, you need to go."

The agent ignored him. He looked around the room, staring at each agent in turn. When Martin's gaze met his, Hagen didn't flinch away. "What's going on here? Why aren't you out there making an arrest, huh? Come on, what are you all sitting on your asses for?"

Caleb was immediately on his feet. "Martin, I—"

Martin slammed both fists on the table, breaking Slade's grip. "I want that bastard *caught*. I want whoever did this dragged in here and strung up. Just put me in a room with him for five minutes. Get out there. Find him. And give me five damn minutes!"

His face flushed red, and his dark eyes bulged in their sockets.

Slade grabbed his upper arm, none too gently this time, and pulled him toward the door. "Caleb, get him home."

Caleb followed, not stopping to say goodbye to the rest of the team or wish them luck in the investigation.

But when they reached the doorway, Martin shook himself out of Slade's grip and jammed his hands against the doorjamb. "None of you are safe," he shouted over his shoulder. "If they killed Jane because of me, they can get to any one of you. You gotta watch your families."

Caleb grabbed one of his arms and, together with Slade, pushed him into the corridor.

Hagen didn't want to admit how much Martin's words shook him. He planned to visit with his sisters—Amanda and Brianna—soon. Right now, he was relieved they lived outside Nashville.

The memory of Jane Lin's body, sprawled on the school stage, her head hacked off, flashed before his eyes. And then Jane's face morphed into Amanda's, then Brianna's.

Ander broke the silence that had fallen over the room. "Anyone think he's right? Anyone think we should be afraid for our families? I mean, if the attack *is* related to our work, then he could be right, couldn't he? Any of our families could be targeted."

No one answered.

Slade came back in. His cheeks were flushed. The storm clouds in his eyes told Hagen that Martin's outburst hadn't left him unmoved. Slade dropped into his chair and rested his elbows on the table.

He addressed Ander. "I heard you out there. The message the killer left on the wall suggests there *might* be a connection to our work. But we can't say for sure, so no one panic. The killer might have been taunting Martin simply because he's an FBI agent."

"But how did the killer know that?" Ander pressed the issue. "If the killer did his research—"

"There're a million ways he could've known about Martin. The simplest explanation is that Jane confronted the killer with the information during their interaction. Then the killer chose to capitalize on it and wrote a threatening message. It might not actually mean *anything*."

That made sense. Jane could have very well thrown her brother's FBI weight around during the confrontation. But just in case...

Slade was reading his mind. "But just in case, I've tried to get some extra protection for our families. As you know, there are always staff shortages, budget constraints, and so on. In short, there are too many of us and not enough of a reason to assign guards to everyone."

Chloe pressed her hands flat on the table, her fingers

spread. She looked as though she were about to leap out of her seat and catch something with her talons. "So we're supposed to just sit here and do nothing? I'm supposed to wait for some killer to follow my wife home from work with an axe?"

"Emphasis will be placed on family members in Nashville because probability dictates this person will stay local. But..." Slade's reassuring expression turned grim. "The safety of our families is up to us. Each of us. I, for one, will make sure my home is secure, my wife and daughters are safe, and they don't open the door to anyone. I suggest you each do the same for your loved ones."

Hagen thought of his own home, empty except for his dog, Bubs. Knowing he had no wife or children to worry about was a strange and sad kind of relief.

Ander rubbed his forehead with the back of his hand. "Thank Christ Murphy's up north."

This was the first time Hagen ever heard Ander express gratitude for the distance between him and his son.

Chloe offered a humorless smile. "You're lucky you're so hard to live with, Ander. Some of us aren't."

Stacy nodded sharply, reminding Hagen of a nanny from British television. "I have family in the city too. Maybe I should tell them to hire extra security. Yes, I think I'll tell them."

Slade addressed the entire room. "The best extra security is to catch this bastard. The quicker we lock him up, the better we'll all feel."

"Or *her*." Stella raised her head. "The quicker we lock *her* up. The killer might actually be a woman."

Hagen wondered what she thought about family protection. The only vulnerable family member Stella had in Nashville was her goldfish.

Chloe frowned. "Why do you say that?"

"Dan...Dan Garcia, the detective, my old partner in the Nashville PD. He thought he found a boot print. It's small. So either a small man or maybe a woman. The print didn't match Martin's sister's shoes. He said it was smaller. This is all very preliminary, but we can't eliminate anyone right now."

Stacy raised her hand but didn't wait to be called on before speaking. "Some studies have shown that women are more likely to use weapons of opportunity. Was there anything in the method that suggested a woman did this?"

"Maybe. Jane was..." She glanced at the door, then lowered her voice in case Martin was still near the conference room. "She was decapitated with a sharp instrument. An axe or hatchet."

Stacy drew her eyebrows together. "A school wouldn't have an axe or hatchet lying around, right? So the killer may have brought it with them. That'd be more in line with a male perpetrator."

Stella glanced at Hagen. "One of the neighbors is missing an axe. Anne Lawson." Across the table, Mac started typing on her laptop, and Hagen knew the cyber sleuth was already hunting down Anne Lawson's records before Stella could finish her thought. "Someone could've easily grabbed it."

"Lawson *says* she's missing an axe. We can't prove she does or doesn't have one." Hagen considered the distance between Anne Lawson's home and the school. It was less than a block. "But you're right. If Lawson had one in the yard, it would've been easy to swipe."

"And the killer needed multiple blows. That could indicate someone with limited upper body strength." Stella seemed to be warming to the killer woman notion.

"Or just someone bad at their job," Stacy countered.

The room was silent for a moment. Hagen recalled the sight of the body, the puddle of blood on the stage, the head staring blankly across the room. He swallowed hard, trying to stop seeing his own sisters' heads rolling around on a dirty floor in an abandoned building.

Mac gave a little *aha*! "Anne Lawson has no criminal history, but she did file a missing persons report about five years ago. Her husband disappeared, supposedly last seen with a woman of Asian descent. He hasn't been seen since."

Hagen thought about the rows of booze bottles. "And she's definitely a regular at liquor stores."

Slade stepped up to the whiteboard and started writing details down. "That's something. Let's dig into Lawson. What else we got?"

Stacy raised her hand. Hagen hid an amused smile. Despite the gravity of the situation, Stacy's mannerisms were proper...and amusing. "Jane Lin's blood was confirmed on the piano tuning hammer. That was probably the initial attack."

Stella thought out loud. "So Jane leaves the liquor store, gets ambushed—"

"Which is in line with a male perpetrator," Stacy interrupted.

"But the piano tuner definitely seems like a weapon of opportunity," Stella countered. "The perpetrator may have found it in the alley...or already had it available."

Mac shifted away from her laptop. "We looked at piano tuners in the city. None had criminal records and very few were women."

"But we do know another woman with a link to pianos." Stella lifted her cast. "Boris Kerne's daughter. And she has good reason to hate the FBI." Her dark eyes settled on Hagen. "She might want revenge. That stuff's like poison."

He kept his face expressionless as the memory of their previous conversation twisted his guts.

Stacy leaned back in her chair, her expressive face giving

every thought away. "Ah, yes. An FBI agent kills her father, and she wants to inflict the same emotional damage on the people who hurt her."

"I don't buy it." Hagen leaned forward. He wasn't going to take the accusatory bullets flying at him. "Kerne was armed, with hostages, and had already taken a shot."

Before Stella could respond, Stacy raised her hand again. And once again, she spoke before anyone could call on her. "But it was her *dad*. Boris Kerne took revenge for a few people falling asleep at a *concert*. If they have a similar mental predisposition, Lisa Kerne might behave much like her father did for a perceived slight."

Slade cleared his throat. "Stella, you and Hagen go and talk to Lisa Kerne. See if you can rule her out. Chloe, give that footprint expert a call. What was her name? Lindy Brown. Mac, Stacy, I want you two to stay here and see what else you can find out about Anne Lawson. I want to know what happened to her husband. Ander, head over to Martin's. Maybe you and Caleb can dig up some information about his sister that could help us. Go."

The team rose. Hagen dug into his pocket for his car keys. When he looked up, Stella was no longer sitting opposite him. She was at the front of the room, approaching Slade.

She spoke quietly, but Hagen was able to make out her words. "Boss, do you mind if I have a quick word?"

Slade nodded.

Hagen watched the two of them leave the room without him.

18

Stella followed Slade to his office at the end of the corridor.

The SSA's office was fairly typical, with no extraneous signs that this was a supervisor's space. His black desk held a monitor, a keyboard, and a half-drunk mug of coffee. His window faced the highway. On a cabinet under the window stood two framed pictures of Slade's wife and his two teenage daughters. The girls grinned behind his back, the youngest's upper teeth hidden by a row of braces.

Slade took a seat and waved at the chair opposite. "What can I do for you?"

Stella sat down, adjusted the seat, tried again, then decided no matter what she did with the chair, this conversation was never going to be comfortable.

In her imagination, this admission was the last step before her final victory. Now that she was here, though, she wasn't sure what to expect. Life had shown her too many times that the future she'd imagined was rarely the future she got.

Either way, she would no longer be alone after years of

thinking about her father's murder, plotting to track down his killer and make an arrest. Her team was behind her now. With this conversation, Slade could bring the whole force of the FBI to bear. Nothing could withstand that weight.

Certainly not the criminal controlling the corrupt cops of Memphis.

Slade lifted an eyebrow at her continued silence. "Stella?"

He reached for his mug of coffee, sipped, and winced. The cup had been sitting there for a while.

Stella dried her damp palm on the side of her pants and resisted the urge to grab a pencil to scratch under her cast. "Sir, you know my father was killed when I was fourteen years old."

Slade pushed the cup to the side. "Yep. It's all in your file. He was a cop. A sergeant, I believe."

"That's right, sir." Words came a little easier, knowing Slade was familiar with her background. Maybe this wouldn't be a surprise to him. "He had a partner before he was killed. Joel Ramirez." Her cheeks warmed. "I called him Uncle Joel."

"I understand he was killed in the line of duty too. Not long after your father." Slade's light eyes were sympathetic and curious about what she would say next.

"That's right, sir." Stella licked her dry lips. "At least, that's what I thought."

Slade waited for an explanation, letting the silence stretch between them. Waiting was an interview technique—suspects, and humans in general, had a difficult time sitting in expectant silence.

There was no turning back now.

"Before Uncle Joel...before the report of Joel Ramirez's death, he told me that the people who'd killed my dad were corrupt cops."

Slade leaned back in his seat. Behind his left shoulder, his wife smiled from a wicker chair on a porch, a glass of lemonade raised in her hand. She seemed to live in a different world, a quiet, relaxing place Slade left behind every time he came into the office.

"I'm sorry to hear that. Did Ramirez tell you who ordered the hit?"

"No. He was drunk. Barely himself. Fell asleep right after he said it. I didn't know what to think. I...I never saw him again, so I never got a chance to ask him what else he knew."

Slade reached for his coffee again. He touched the cup and frowned. To avoid reaching for it again, he put the cup on the windowsill. Then he turned back to her.

"And you're telling me this now because...?"

"Because he's not dead. Joel Ramirez. Thing is, I've... we've managed to track him down. He's in witness protection under the name—"

Slade lifted a hand. "I don't need to know his name. And Stella, neither do you. How did you find him?"

"I...I had a source." Stella pressed her lips together. Under no circumstances did she want Mac or Mac's source in hot water.

Slade nodded, not pushing her. "And you've spoken to him? This Joel Ramirez. Or whatever his name is."

"No, not yet. We just saw him when—"

"*We?*"

"Me and...and Hagen. He heard what I was doing and wanted to help. Just to watch my back. That kind of thing. We went to Atlanta together. But the cheerleader case broke before we got a chance to confront Joel."

"Mm. That explains why you two took so long to get there."

He locked his gaze on Stella's for several uncomfortable moments. The intensity of his look was the closest Stella had come to a reprimand in the few short weeks she'd been in the FBI.

"Yeah. Sorry, we—"

Slade waved away her apology. "What you do on your day off is your business. And who you do it with. For the most part." He leaned forward, resting his forearms on his desktop. "So what are you going to do now? You've dug into witness protection, possibly put someone in danger, and risked your career as well as a colleague's...and the career of whoever gave you this information. What do you intend to do?"

Stella swallowed. She knew the correct answer was to say she was going to do nothing. Admit she'd been foolish and promise to step back and leave Joel Ramirez safely in the hands of witness protection.

And if she wasn't going to do that—and she *wasn't*—she should lie and say she was going to do nothing.

"I...I'm going to speak to Joel Ramirez. I need to know who gave the order."

"I could pass your information on to the Memphis police if you want. This should be their investigation, after all. Their Internal Affairs should deal with it."

Stella shook her head. "No, sir. All I've got is a drunken comment made over a decade ago. And if Uncle...if Joel is in witness protection, there's probably a reason."

"And you think if the Memphis police department has corrupt officers, you don't trust them to handle the investigation."

"Exactly." Stella needed Slade to understand how important, how necessary, this "side investigation" was to her. "My dad trusted these men...or women...and they betrayed him. I need to know what happened. Joel Ramirez might be in danger from them as well. That's probably why he's in witness protection. I need to know if there's something here."

"And if there is something here, Stella? What then?"

"Then, sir, I'm going to bring the bastard in."

Slade seemed to lose himself in thought.

Stella didn't speak. It was her turn to wait him out.

Through the window, cars zoomed down the highway.

In the office, the minutes ticked past.

Eventually, Slade turned back to her. "Knox, you're taking a great risk. I doubt witness protection will look on you speaking to one of their charges kindly. I imagine as soon as you speak to him, he'll be moved. But I understand why you feel the need to do this, so the sooner you get it over with, the better. I have some people I can call. I'll see what I can do to smooth your way."

Stella's heart leapt. "Really, sir? Thank you."

Slade lifted a hand. "But you've got a job to do. We need to find justice for Martin and his sister first. Go grab Hagen and find Lisa Kerne."

19

Hagen waited for Stella in the parking garage, leaning against the side of his Corvette. Sweat ran down his temple and dripped off the end of his jaw, but he didn't move. The sweat had nothing to do with the heat outside.

Stella was with Slade. She was telling him everything. Or almost everything.

His stomach clenched.

Whatever she was blabbing to Slade about would only make his mission harder. But maybe that was the point. Maybe Stella was making sure there were more people watching the target. She was trying to stop him from doing things *his* way.

Dammit.

He pushed himself off the Corvette and paced to the edge of the parking lot. A concrete wall gave him a taller support and distance from the FBI's offices. He wanted to think. He wiped his brow.

Perhaps he was being too hard on her. Stella had never let him down. She didn't agree with what he wanted to do. He knew that. But she believed she could persuade him to do things her way. He saw the plea in her eyes, heard the hope in her voice. Part of her didn't think him capable of killing the killer.

So surely, she wouldn't have told Slade he planned to execute the rat bastard.

She wouldn't have done that.

The agency door opened, and Stella came out. She stopped, lifted a hand to her brow, and scanned the parking garage until she settled on Hagen by the wall.

For a moment, the two of them held eye contact. Nothing in Stella's dark eyes betrayed what she'd done or said in that room.

Hagen pushed the button on the remote control in his pocket. A nearby Bureau vehicle beeped, and the lights flashed twice. Stella crossed the parking lot and walked to the passenger's side. She climbed in without saying a word.

Hagen drove out of the parking lot in silence.

Only when they'd pulled onto I-240 did he ask his question. He tried to keep his voice casual, even though his knuckles were white on the steering wheel.

"What did you tell him?"

Stella kept her eyes on the road. "I told him what I'm doing. And why I'm doing it."

"What does that mean?"

"It means exactly what it means."

"So you told him you want to find the person who ordered your father's murder and—"

"And bring him in. Yes."

Hagen stretched his fingers. Sweat pooled in the palms of his hands. So far, so predictable.

"What did you tell him about me?"

Stella faced him, turning in her seat. "What should I have told him about you?"

He wasn't entirely sure he wanted to answer that question. Stella *should* have told Slade that Hagen wasn't interested in bringing their fathers' killer or killers to justice. He wanted that sonofabitch dead, and he needed to be stopped.

But her question also told him she hadn't said anything to Slade. And that was good news.

He lifted the side of his mouth into a half-smile. "What you *should* have told him is that I'm the FBI's greatest investigator and you think I should get a promotion and a raise."

She relaxed back into her seat. "Damn, knew I forgot something."

"Typical. We can go back if you want."

"I'm good. I'll try to remember next time I see him." Stella adjusted the air-conditioning vent, pushing the cold air away from her face. "I didn't tell him anything about you. I just said you came with me to Atlanta to watch my back. Nothing about your dad or anything like that. That's your business." Her voice was flat, as though Slade's response had been entirely expected, entirely normal. "He said he'd help us if he can."

Slade's involvement would complicate matters. The more people who knew what Stella was doing, the greater the chance someone might stop Hagen. But if Slade didn't know the depths of his involvement, if he wasn't aware of Hagen's own plan, he'd have more freedom.

The new restrictions weren't enough to stop him.

20

Nailing and drilling echoed through the high foyer of the Kentwood Philharmonic. The noise competed with the gentler sound of piano music from the auditorium beyond, and it was winning.

Though nearly two weeks had passed since Stella was last here, work on the philharmonic's new offices still wasn't finished. Stella was starting to believe the renovation was a never-ending task. As soon as the construction was done, the philharmonic's director—the sleek, efficient Amy Cooper—would head back to the cocktail parties and fundraising dinners to collect more checks and start again. That was, after all, her job.

Stella led the way through the building, with Hagen following close behind. They'd guessed, based on the time of day, that they'd have a better chance of catching Lisa Kerne here rather than at her house.

Déjà vu hit her hard as they stepped into the auditorium.

The last time she'd been here, she and Ander had come to question Lisa about a series of murders in Kentwood related to the philharmonic.

She and Ander had agreed to the director's request to wait until the show ended. They'd sat in a box and watched the performance. For nearly two hours, Stella forgot about the case. She didn't think about her father's murder. As Lisa Kerne played like a virtuoso through the program, she almost forgot killers roamed the streets, trawling for new victims. At the concert, time stood still.

It was the most pleasant evening Stella had enjoyed in a very long time.

Since then, Hagen had killed Lisa's father.

Stella ran her hand over the cast on her left wrist. The busted wrist and rib were mementos from her run-in with the man.

Would Lisa be capable of murder if push came to shove? Stella herself knew how far a daughter would go to see justice for her father.

Beside her, Hagen eyed the empty seats. She glanced at him, taking in his square jaw and clean-cut looks. No one would suspect the vengeful fire simmering beneath his surface. Stella swallowed hard against a sudden lump in her throat.

Was Lisa Kerne more of a justice seeker, like her?

Or was she more vengeful, like Hagen?

Onstage, a single spotlight illuminated an empty chair and music stand. The piano stood in the shadows where Lisa Kerne played, as if she wanted to be nowhere near the circle of light.

The pianist leaned her head over one shoulder, revealing the band of shaved scalp above her right ear. She looked more like a goth teenager than a full-grown woman. The chains of her long silver earrings swayed as her fingers jumped up and down the keyboard. She wore black combat boots.

"Ravel," Hagen whispered. "His *Sérénade Grotesque*. My

piano teacher tried to get me to play it once. It's really hard."

Although she was only halfway down the stairs, Stella stopped and listened. Lisa was a world-class pianist...much better than her father. It was difficult to ignore her talent.

The rapid beats the pianist played at the beginning of the piece faded into a gentle melody. Lisa Kerne stroked the keys as though she were petting the head of a kitten.

And then she was off again. Her hands bouncing up and down like a cat toying with a mouse's tail.

Clang.

Stella flinched at the discordant note.

"Damn, damn, *damn!*" Lisa beat on her keyboard, filling the hall with a series of loud, random chords.

Stella's eyebrows rose in surprise. That was a lot of frustration for a missed note.

She continued down the stairs. "Lisa Kerne?"

Lisa's dark hair whipped around. For a moment, a look of confusion spread across her face, but it passed quickly. Her back sagged, and she rested her hands on her legs when she recognized Stella.

"You again."

Stella climbed a small set of steps onto the stage. Hagen followed. Their footsteps echoed through the auditorium as they approached the piano.

Lisa's eyes narrowed.

She examined Hagen, eyeing him from head to toe, as though she were checking a rental car for dents. Her scrutiny stopped at his face, and her eyes widened ever so slightly. She turned back to Stella, her gaze lingering on Hagen even as she moved her head.

Stella realized it might be a mistake to have Hagen, the man who shot and killed Lisa's father, present. Or maybe not. Her reaction could be telling.

"What do you want from me now? My father's dead.

Justice was served. What more could you *possibly* want?"

Lisa's voice sounded tired, as though just thinking about her father sucked away her energy. And Stella couldn't blame her. How could she take more from Lisa than they'd taken already?

"We're working on a new case and need to speak with you. Nothing to do with your father."

Lisa closed her eyes and exhaled deeply. "Another case. Aren't you lucky, Agent Knox? The fun stuff just keeps on flowing for you."

Hagen drew up next to the piano. He ran a hand over the instrument's black sides, which shone in the auditorium's lights. "Wouldn't really call this stuff fun. Music? That's fun. Murder? Not so much. It's a serious business."

Lisa's lips curled at the corners. "Who are you?"

For a moment Stella felt a brief sense of relief. Lisa didn't recognize Hagen from the news. "And what happened to the other guy? Special Agent Big Hair?"

Hagen dipped into his pocket and removed his ID. "I'm Special Agent Hagen Yates. By the other guy, I'm guessing you mean Special Agent Ander Bennett. He's busy. You've got me today."

"Do I?" Lisa took the ID and read it closely. She read his name aloud, almost singing the words from the badge. "Hagen Yates. FBI. Well, it's nice to get you, Special Agent Hagen Yates. I dare say you've heard all about me by now."

Hagen retrieved his ID from Lisa's grip. "I wouldn't say I've heard *all* about you. Heard a few things, though."

Lisa twisted in her chair and ran her fingers over the keyboard, creating a melody Stella didn't recognize. She held her finger on the last note.

"All good, I hope?"

Hagen pocketed his ID card. "It was certainly all interesting. I hear you're very talented."

Lisa bounced a finger on one of the keys.

Bing. Bing. Bing.

"I'll take interesting and talented. Something interesting is sure to happen."

Stella came around the piano stool. Lisa now had Hagen on one side and Stella on the other, hemming her in.

Stella pulled out her notebook. "Lisa, do you know a Jane Lin?"

Lisa reached for the last black key on her left, forcing Stella to step back from the keyboard. The C-sharp released a long, deep, ominous *bong*.

"Can't say that I do, Agent Knox. You want to try another one?"

Hagen stepped in. "I'll try one. Where were you last night?"

Lisa tinkled the last three keys on the right, pushing Hagen backward.

Ding, ding, ding.

"Out."

"Out where?"

"Out. That's where."

Stella moved closer again, blocking off the bottom octave on the keyboard. "Lisa, we're conducting a murder inquiry. You need to—"

"Another one?" Lisa dropped her hands into her lap. "My, you are busy there in the FBI, aren't you? I wasn't out visiting my dad if that's why you're asking. You killed him, remember?"

She looked from Stella to Hagen and held her gaze on Agent Yates for an awkward moment before shifting back to Stella.

It wasn't clear whether Lisa was accusing the two of them directly, or the FBI in general. She thought of the chalked message on the crime scene stage wall.

Chop, chop, FBI.

Lisa's attitude could be grief...or anger. She'd been prickly before. Now, she seemed tired.

Each time Stella had lost someone, she'd barely found the energy to leave her room, let alone hack someone's head off. But maybe Lisa was tired because she'd been *out* chopping a head off last night. She decided to offer a gentler approach. "I'm sorry for your loss. Really, I am. It's not easy to lose a father. You must—"

"No, it isn't," Lisa snapped. "Especially when you've hardly seen your father for years, barely saw him when you were growing up, and you've already lost your mother. Not easy to lose your father at all."

Stella nodded. "I understand."

"Do you? I doubt you do, Agent Knox. I really do."

"My father was killed in the line of duty. He was a police officer. I might understand more than you think."

She narrowed her eyes. "Was he shot?"

"Yes."

Lisa folded her hands into her lap and fixed her gaze on Hagen, dismissing Stella's sympathetic attempts. "My father taught me everything I know about music. He was my only friend and my only family. He needed help, and you people killed him." She shot Stella a daggered glance. "You don't understand shit."

"I'm sorry you feel that way. But we still need to know your whereabouts last night."

"I stopped by a music store downtown around eight o'clock. Then I grabbed a coffee. Then I went home. I played Rachmaninoff. Then some Beethoven. The classics."

"You practice a lot." Hagen turned to face the keyboard. He played a single chord, holding down three keys with his right hand. Lisa waited for the chord to die before slamming the keyboard lid closed, just missing the tips of Hagen's fingers as he whisked them away.

"One has to stay sharp, Agent Yates. Now, do you have any more questions?"

Stella, a bit angry at Lisa's dismissal of her own loss, leaned against the closed piano lid. "Yes. Which music store did you go to last night?"

Lisa narrowed her eyes. "Well, it certainly wasn't the one where you murdered my father."

Hagen paled, but his face gave nothing else away. "Then which one?"

"I told you, the one downtown."

Stella knew which one she meant, so she changed the subject. "Do you own a piano tuning hammer?"

Lisa gave a small, scoffing laugh. "Do I own a piano tuning hammer? Are you having trouble with your piano, Agent Knox? I can recommend a tuner if you want. He's very good."

Hagen pressed a finger into the piano lid's polished surface. It left a clear fingerprint. "So you don't tune your own piano?"

"Do I look like a piano tuner? I'm a pianist, Agent Hagen Yates. I do not own a piano tuning hammer. You can buy one in a good music store if you're interested. Now, again, do you have any more questions? Because if you don't, I really need to practice, and they're going to need the auditorium soon. They're looking for a new cellist. Maybe someone in the FBI would like to audition for a proper job?"

"What did you buy, then?" Stella asked.

Lisa waved a hand. "I didn't find what I was looking for."

Stella couldn't resist a small dig at the unpleasant woman. "You playing a new piece? Sounded like you were struggling a little as we came in."

Lisa glared at her. "Not new. Just…you know, I just lost

my father. Not easy to focus when you're mourning."

Hagen slipped his hands into his pockets. "Especially when the father you lost just killed three people, then a couple more, and finally two others. Before holding people hostage in a music store."

Lisa threw open the piano lid and faced the keyboard. "Do you have another question or not?"

Hagen rocked on his heels. "Yeah. Can I borrow your shoes?"

Two minutes later, they stood outside the auditorium, and Lisa Kerne was still on the stage, still wearing her boots.

"We could have done that better." Stella yanked the SUV's passenger door open. "We might have come away with permission to take her shoes for testing."

Hagen shook his head as he climbed behind the wheel. "No, we wouldn't have. She was never going to give us permission, and we're not going to get a warrant, not with what we've got."

Stella strapped in. The vehicle had roasted in the sun outside the philharmonic building, and after the over-revved air-conditioning of the auditorium, Stella felt like she'd stepped into an oven.

"We do have a lot of circumstantial evidence, though. A link to pianos at the site of the abduction. A possible woman's shoe print. Lisa Kerne has small feet. And she's the daughter of a killer we've just killed. 'Chop, chop, FBI.' She's talking to us."

Hagen gunned the engine and flipped the air-conditioning to maximum. "Sounds like you're thinking like father like daughter."

"Both seem pretty vengeful." She refused to glance directly at Hagen as she said this. "But if she is like her father, we're going to need more than a hatred of the Feds and some major daddy issues for evidence to take her down."

21

Sis jogged through the park, heading through the gate and out along the sidewalk until she was about ten yards from the home of Hagen Yates.

A delivery truck drove up the road, and Sis slowed to let it pass. Only when the vehicle turned the corner and was out of sight did she race up the townhome's empty driveway. Stopping just before she reached the backyard, Sis rested her hands on her knees and breathed heavily.

She was hidden from the road, unseen behind the wall separating his yard from the neighbor's. Her breathing slowed.

Still crouched, she pulled her phone out of her running pack and clicked on the camera. She eased the lens around the corner of the house. The screen showed Hagen's concrete patio. A pair of sunbeds stretched under the roof.

Neither of the sunbeds had a cushion. Judging by the layer of dust covering both of them, Hagen had little time to lie in the sun and work on his tan.

He also didn't seem to care much about his yard. Weeds

grew between cracks in the concrete, and paint peeled from some of the pickets in his fence.

Why have such a fancy house if you just let it fall into disrepair?

Sis re-angled the phone to view the patio door. And there, just below the eaves of the roof, was the security camera.

She removed a small compact from her pack, opened it, wiped the mirror, and placed it on the ground. Adjusting the mirror until the sun reflected off it just right, she smiled as a small white circle struck the side of the house and stretched, forming an oval about six inches long.

Sis adjusted the mirror until the reflection reached the corner of the eaves. One slight movement of the mirror and the circle of light shined directly into the security camera lens. The light would essentially blind the camera…but not for long.

In about three minutes, the sun would move enough that the light would slide away and reveal anyone standing at the door.

Sis hoped three minutes were enough.

She hurried to the patio door and pulled her lock picks out of her pouch. "Dammit," she muttered. "Should have brought a bigger pouch. A pick gun would have been through this lock in seconds."

Dipping back into her running pack, Sis pulled out a pair of thin leather gloves and put them on. They were soft and pliable from years of careful treatment. The gloves prevented fingerprints without compromising ease of movement for detail work…like lock picking.

Carefully, Sis slipped the tension wrench into the lock and twisted. The lock moved less than a millimeter and stopped. She maintained just enough pressure to hold the driver pins above the shear line. With her other hand, she took the rake pick and scrubbed the inside of the lock. One pin clicked, then another. The lock turned again, then a little more.

Yes, c'mon.

The chamber held. Sis increased the tension. Still nothing.

Shit. Feels like two more pins left. C'mon.

Above her, more than half the circle of reflected light had already passed the lens. Sis licked her lips. A bead of sweat escaped the bottom of her sunglasses and crawled across her cheek.

With one hand holding the tension wrench and the other gripping the rake pin, she could do no more than wipe her face on her shoulder.

She raked again. Nothing.

Nuts. Come on. Slowly now.

Again, she dragged the pick back and forth inside the lock, feeling the pins rise and fall with a gentle click.

Still, the chamber didn't move.

Easy. Take it easy. You're applying too much pressure. Relax.

She glanced at the security camera again. A sliver of light still shined directly into the lens. If some guard somewhere was actually watching that thing, once the light moved clear, they'd see her standing at the door with a bag of lock picks and a frustrated look. She'd stand out like a barn dancer on a ballet stage.

One more time.

She eased the tension in her left hand and raked again with her right.

Backward, forward, backward again. The light slipped along the lens. Another drop of sweat rolled down her cheek and…*click*.

The lock turned. Sis stepped into Hagen's kitchen, closing the door behind her just as the light slid off the lens and struck the eaves of the roof.

She wiped the sweat from her brow, breathed out slowly, and pushed her tools back into her pack.

A deep, threatening growl greeted her.

Sis froze.

A dog stood in the kitchen doorway.

The beast looked like a cross between a pit bull and a boxer. His shoulders were as wide and muscular as a pork loin, and the creature's black eyes were fixed firmly on Sis.

She swallowed.

She'd met Hagen and his dog in the park, but she wasn't sure the animal would remember her. He'd seemed tired but friendly then. However, crossing into a dog's territory was a different situation than meeting them in a park.

Bubs, that was the creature's name—short for Bubbles.

A dog named Bubbles couldn't be very threatening.

Carefully, little by little, Sis lowered herself to her haunches. She held out her arm and offered the dog the back of her hand, letting him sniff the leather of her gloves. Her voice was calm and quiet, almost singsongy.

"Hey, Bubs. How are you doing today? You remember me, right?"

Hagen's dog panted heavily. His jaw fell open, revealing long lines of saliva and a row of teeth as sharp and jagged as a bed of nails.

Sis didn't move. Her throat was as dry as straw.

If the dog wasn't as stupid as he looked, she was going to be in big trouble. Slowly, she pushed a hand into her running pack.

Her fingers landed on the grip of her little Beretta Pico. She stopped. That was certainly one option. But a beast like that could have her arm off before she'd finished aiming. The shot would alert the neighbors, and a dead dog would alert Hagen Yates and the entire FBI.

There was no room for error.

Bubs licked his lips.

Sis pushed her fingers deeper into her running pack. She reached past her weapon and found the dog treat, pulling it out slowly, extending her arm.

The dog lifted one heavy paw and took half a step forward, then another. Cautiously, as if waiting for Sis to make one false move, Bubs approached her hand. He sniffed, then took the treat, flapping his long pink tongue all the way up past her wrist.

"Aww, Bubs. You greasy little monkey."

The dog chewed and swallowed with a loud *harumph*, dropped onto his back, and waved his legs in the air.

Sis rubbed his tummy.

"You haven't changed, have you? Even when someone breaks into your home, you just roll right over."

With one hand still on the dog's tummy, Sis lifted her sunglasses and looked around the kitchen.

The place was abnormally clean, as though Hagen had prepared his house for a *Better Homes & Gardens* magazine shoot. The kettle stood at the back of the counter, its spout facing forward like a soldier on guard. The chrome of the coffee machine sparkled. Even the dark window of the microwave was entirely free of fingerprints and smears.

Leaving Bubs to beg for more belly scratches, she opened the fridge.

Here, too, was a world of unrestrained order.

The milk and orange juice cartons stood shoulder to shoulder in the door. Bottles of beer, with labels pointing outward, were arranged in a row on the bottom shelf of the door. Three plastic containers with printed labels reading *Wanja Jeon*, *Rainbow Rice*, and *Chicken Curry* took up space on the middle shelf.

Sis pulled out the box of curry, removed the lid, and pushed a finger into the orange goop inside. She removed her finger and sucked hard. Replacing the lid, she nodded at Bubs.

"Not a bad cook, your master." She lowered her voice. "But you can tell him he's a wuss when it comes to spice."

She strode into the living room.

The sight of a sofa with mustard-yellow canvas cushions surprised her. She'd figured Hagen to be a La-Z-Boy kind of guy, all upholstered recliner and space on the arm for a chilled beer. At most, he'd have one of those leather sofas that reeked of seduction and money. This was all too homey, too comfortable. Hagen Yates shouldn't have a living room like this, not until he had a wife with two kids and a job in insurance.

Sis approached the shelf beneath the wall-mounted television. The domesticity of the room continued.

A line of framed photographs stretched across his mantel, each picture angled to exactly the same degree. Most of the pictures showed three women, each with Hagen's square chin and dark green eyes.

Energy from one of the young women beamed beyond the frame as she gripped her high school diploma.

Another picture showed a young woman leaping a hedge on the back of a horse. Her body was bent over the horse's neck. Her long brown hair flew over her shoulder beneath her riding hat.

Next to her was a photograph of an older woman with short brown curls shot with gray. The picture must have been taken at a Thanksgiving dinner because she was beaming over a roast turkey, its skin crisp and brown.

A picture in the middle of the shelf drew Sis's attention. The face that filled the frame showed a middle-aged man. His hair was combed to the left, revealing the beginning of a widow's peak. His mustache was thick but neatly trimmed.

Sis lifted the picture from the shelf. "So this is Seth Yates."

She cocked her head and sized him up. "Can see where your boy gets his looks. Bit of a hottie, weren't you, Seth? The Officer certainly didn't like you."

She held onto the picture. She'd heard a lot about Seth Yates. How he could find a legal loophole the size of a needle's eye, make a jury weep for the meanest, dirtiest gangbanger, negotiate plea deals that would make district attorneys beg for his client's signature. He'd done so well...until he didn't do so well.

Taking a case for a rival was just greedy. And getting that drug lord off...well, now, that was unforgivable.

"Lie with dogs, get fleas, Seth. And sometimes, you wake up to find your head's been bitten off."

She slid the photo back onto the shelf, adjusting the angle until the frame was exactly in its place.

Bubs followed her upstairs and into what she assumed was Hagen's bedroom. His closet contained drawers of neatly rolled ties, pressed shirts arranged by color, and jackets all facing the same direction on their hangers.

Hagen had turned the spare room into a gym where the weights were piled neatly, and the exercise bike faced the window and the street below. A cabinet in the corner held files of receipts and folders of paid bills.

Sis put her hands on her hips and rolled a foot over a dumbbell. "Jesus, Hagen, are you an FBI agent or an accountant?"

She made her way back downstairs, Bubs at her heels. A smoke alarm was directly above the coffee table. Sis slipped off her shoes, stood on the table, and removed the cover.

The bug she fitted into the space next to the battery wasn't the best, but the microphone was strong enough to catch a conversation anywhere in the living room or kitchen.

She sat on the corner of the table, retied her shoes, and

pulled out her phone. As the line rang, Bubs rested his big head in her lap. She scratched the dog between his ears.

"You stupid mutt."

"What you say?" The voice on the phone was angry and sharp.

Sis swallowed. "Not you, hun. Just got a stupid dog here. I'm at the house. I put in a device but there's nothing here. No papers or notebook or nothing. Tell you one thing, though."

"What's that?"

"Guy still thinks about his dad. Got his picture front and center on his mantelpiece."

The phone was silent for a moment. "Is that right?"

"Kinda hard to miss. And there's something about this guy. I don't know…he's too neat, too cool. And he was quick to shoot on his last case too. Reminds me of myself a little. I'm starting to think we need to keep a closer eye on him than on our Stella Knox."

22

Some people liked to end their week in a bar or a club. I always preferred Bernie's Books, a small two-story bookstore on Avon Street in Kentwood.

I sat in the café on the ground floor, near the classic literature section, which opened into the children's section. I'd collected my tea, which came in a small white pot with a cup and a saucer—as it should—and I'd piled three books in front of me on the table.

All were versions of *Alice in Wonderland*.

One was a recently published pop-up book, the text of the story truncated and replaced with cutouts of Alice and the Cheshire Cat and the Queen of Hearts. They leapt from the book, ready to scratch my hand and chop off my head as I turned the pages.

Another was a new compendium, combining the two Alice books and adding an introduction from some professor of literature at Berkeley. She discussed narrative and meta-narrative and the symbology of maturity in the books as though I, Lewis Carroll, or anyone else gave a damn.

The third book was the one that interested me the most.

It didn't promise anything new. On the contrary, the cover had been designed to look old. Running my finger over the embossed gold lettering on the front, I imagined myself sitting in some oak-paneled library, enjoying a view of my estate, while waiting to hear that the order to execute my enemies had been carried out.

But I wasn't reading any of those books. They were just keeping me company.

I sipped my tea and searched my phone for information about one FBI Special Agent Hagen Yates.

The internet gave me very little. There was a home inspector in Philadelphia with the same name. A guitar teacher called Hagen Yates offered a first lesson for free. There was even a nuclear weapons inspector, a former Air Force officer with a soft face.

"Excuse me."

A little girl with long blond hair, wearing a pink t-shirt with a unicorn, stood at my elbow. She was probably about nine years old. Approaching me demonstrated she had the confidence of someone twice her age. She didn't even wait for me to respond.

"Are you finished with that?"

She pointed at the *Alice in Wonderland* pop-up book next to the teapot. It was hard to miss. The book was about four inches thick, with uneven cardboard pages.

"This one?" I opened the book to the middle. There was Alice standing upright beneath an arc of flying playing cards. She was almost alive, almost moving.

"Yes, please."

I closed the book. "No."

The little girl stood there for a moment, her big brown eyes surprised. When I continued to ignore her, she dragged her feet back to her mother, who waited at the next table to stroke her hair and provide consolation.

I returned to my phone and adjusted my filters.

FBI. Hagen Yates. Tennessee. News.

The most recent report was in *The Tennessean* with the headline "World Famous Pianist Takes Hostages."

I picked up my tea and swallowed, even though it was still hot. The liquid burned down my suddenly tight throat, but I welcomed the heat.

Steeling myself, I read the article. One sentence practically leapt from the page.

"Kerne died on the scene. FBI Special Agent Hagen Yates is currently under investigation for the officer-involved shooting which brought the hostage situation to a close."

I went back to the main search results, scrolling faster now.

At the bottom of the page was a link to a Memphis newspaper. The story was nearly fifteen years old, covering the murder of a lawyer, Seth Yates. He'd been shot to death on some courthouse steps. The reporter suggested gangland shenanigans.

Seth Yates had upset the wrong people, the reporter mused. He'd paid for his mistake with his life. The last line of the article said Seth Yates was survived by his wife and three children, Brianna, Amanda, and Hagen.

I copied Brianna's name and pasted it into the search engine.

"Excuse me, you're *not* reading that book. You're looking at your *phone*."

The blond girl had returned. She stood with hands on her hips and her face contorted into the cutest scowl I'd ever seen. It made me want to laugh. "Do you like *Alice in Wonderland?*"

She nodded. "It's my favorite book in the whole wide world."

"Is it? Do you like the Queen of Hearts?"

The girl shrugged. She probably preferred Alice or the White Rabbit. Most kids did.

"Do you know what the Queen of Hearts likes to do more than anything in the world?"

The girl shook her head. "No, and I don't care. I just want that book if you're not—"

"She likes to chop off people's heads. Chop, chop." I leaned closer and lowered my voice. "And if you don't fuck off, I'll chop off your head. And your mother's."

The precocious little gnat kept her horror-ridden gaze steady on my face as she backed away. Only when she'd retreated half the distance to her table did she turn and run the rest.

I opened the search results and smiled.

23

Lisa Kerne's rendition of Ravel circled in Hagen's head as they drove back from Kentwood. He couldn't quite remember the tune Boris Kerne had played during the hostage situation, but the constant tinkling of keys brought him back to that moment. He stood before the piano. His gun raised.

Boris Kerne's face morphed in his imagination, transforming to the faceless man who shot his own father.

Hagen remembered the small resistance of the trigger under his finger. It had pulled back so smoothly.

Boris had fallen before him.

The same way his father's murderer would fall before him.

He mentally shook his head, trying to push the tune out of his mind. With Stella sitting right beside him, he didn't want to dwell on these thoughts. She might pick up on something…off.

Hagen shifted through radio stations. Country, classic rock, even some far-too-lively Mexican flashed across the airwaves but didn't match either his or Stella's mood.

Eventually, he gave up and turned to his classic piano Spotify list. The gentle sound of Satie tinkled under the roar of the SUV's engine.

"Damn. Never took you for the quiet piano bar type."

"You never took me at all." His cheeks warmed as he added hastily, softening the comment, "Not to a piano bar or anywhere else."

"We were supposed to do Korean once, remember? Maybe next time."

Next time.

That sounded good to Hagen.

In Atlanta, they'd planned to eat in a Korean restaurant near the hotel. If Stella was talking about visiting that restaurant, they were going back to Atlanta. They'd hunt down Joel Ramirez.

Together.

"Sounds good. *Bibimbap*'s on me."

As they pulled into the parking garage at the Resident Agency, the music changed. Satie fell away to be replaced by the repeated, catchy *bom-ba-da-da-da* of Ravel's *Boléro*. Hagen rolled his eyes. "I am never getting Ravel out of my head."

They climbed out and headed toward the building.

"You know what could help you?" Stella held the door open for him.

"With this damn earworm? What's that?"

"Listening to something else."

"You think that will get this noise out of my head?"

Stella let the door close behind her and overtook him on the way to the conference room. "It might. Less empty space, less echo."

Slade slipped past them, appearing from nowhere. Sometimes, the SSA was like a ghost. "All right, you two. Good to see you're bonding so well. Take your seats. Day's coming to an end, and we've still got a lot to do."

Hagen took a quick head count as he sat down. "Ander not back yet?"

Slade pushed a notepad onto the table. "He's staying at Martin's. Digging into Jane's background. Maybe there was something in her New York life that could have made her a target. That message to the Feds could have concerned a case *she* worked on rather than us."

Hagen's eyebrows rose. "You think so?"

"No. But we needed to check every possibility. Ander's talked to New York. Most of Jane's clients were smalltime, petty criminals with no underworld connections. Frankly, her clients were the kind of people who struggled to get out of their own neighborhoods, let alone come all the way down here to avenge a six-month suspended sentence. Ander's trying to find out about Jane's private life."

Mac turned her phone in her hand, seeming to wish it would provide her some answers. "Good luck finding out private stuff from her *brother*. The only thing I ever told my brothers about my private life is what would happen to them if they ever poked their noses into it."

Hagen grinned. "Then you told them you've got a private life worth poking a nose into. If my sisters threatened me like that, I'd start becoming best friends with their best friends."

Mac wrinkled her nose. "Guess my brothers just weren't as nosy as you."

"Must not've cared enough." He winked at her.

"And your sisters are willing to put up with a lot more crap from their brother than I would."

"Hey, I take plenty of crap from them. I let my little sister name my dog Bubbles."

A couple chuckles sounded from around the room.

More serious, Hagen leaned forward, resting his forearms on the table. "But it's my job to look out for them. Make sure they never meet the kind of people we meet. So yes, I'll read a diary page or two."

Slade drummed his palm on the table, pulling their attention back to the situation at hand. "Chloe, what did you find out about the footprint?"

Chloe scratched the back of her neck. "Not much. Lindy agrees the print probably comes from a woman's shoe, and it was probably made recently. But she pointed out the place is open to the public. With no shoes to compare the print to, there's not much more she can tell me."

"Maybe we could take the neighbor's shoes?" Hagen asked. "Anne Lawson. If we get a match there, we're made."

Slade shook his head. "On what grounds?"

"She…" Hagen stopped and searched for a reason. Nothing he could think of came close. "She owns or once owned an axe."

"So do I." Slade threw up his hands. "Do I look like an axe murderer?"

Chloe laughed. "Maybe in the right light. When the paperwork is late."

Slade ignored her. "You want to tell the judge that Lawson *may* have owned an axe, Hagen, you let me know. I'll buy the popcorn."

"But we shouldn't be ruling her out," Hagen countered. "She's close. She drinks. Her husband's missing for chrissakes, lost to some Asian woman, and she's…she's weird."

Chloe grinned. "You tell that to the judge, I think we're going to need a lot of popcorn."

Everyone laughed.

Hagen joined them.

He knew, as soon as he'd landed on "weird," that mockery would follow.

"Okay, enough." Slade lifted a hand. "This is serious business, and Hagen has a point. Mac, what have you found out about her missing husband?"

Mac frowned. "Still waiting on the detective on his missing persons case to call me back. I'll let you know as soon as I hear from him."

Slade didn't seem pleased. "Keep digging. We need everything you can find on her missing husband. Is he really missing? Has he shown up? Or should we be thinking about a warrant to dig up her garden?"

Mac fingers started moving. "On it."

"What else we got?"

Stacy lifted her hand. "I just wanted to say Mac and I were able to obtain lists of all the students and teachers who attended and taught at Merys High School in the ten years before it closed. It's a lot of people, of course. The school was quite large. But we're working through them all and cross-checking criminal records."

"Did you try looking for Lisa Kerne?" Stella's dark eyes were intense.

In that moment, Hagen realized Stella believed the pianist may have actually murdered Martin's sister.

Stacy's cheeks reddened. "Er, no. I…I didn't think…I—"

"No worries. I did." Mac held up a finger. "She's listed."

Stella clapped her hands together. "I knew we were looking in the right direction."

"Hold your horses, Stella. So is Hagen's Anne Lawson. She was a student and then a teaching assistant. In the music department. And get this, before he disappeared, her husband left her for an Asian FBI agent."

Stella's eyebrows shot up. "An FBI agent? Where'd you hear that?"

Mac waved her phone. "Google. His disappearance earned him a brief article in *The Tennessean*. Plus, I read the missing persons report. Seems he ran away with Special Agent Sydney Chan."

"Good. See if you can track Special Agent Chan down, Mac. Give her a call." Slade looked from Hagen to Stella and back again. "But you all know that's not enough to bring either of them in. A lot of people went to that school. And the killer might have no connection to the place at all. They could've just seen an abandoned building as a good place to leave a body."

The room fell silent.

Progress on this case was too slow, in Hagen's opinion. Every step forward came with three-quarters of a step back.

Stella seemed to want some action too. "Let's keep digging into Anne Lawson. But I think we need to tail Lisa Kerne. Something about that piano tuner is bothering me. Lisa has motive, means, and as far as we know, she had the opportunity. It's next to impossible to get any information out of her directly."

Slade rubbed his chin thoughtfully, staring at Stella. The quiet stretched out as he appraised her. Hagen knew the SSA was evaluating Stella's gut against the available evidence. Finally, he lowered his hand. "We'd have to figure out a tail amongst ourselves. I won't get any extra help based on the little we have so far."

"*I* could do it." Chloe's voice was firm, a declaration instead of an appeal.

Slade nodded, but Hagen could tell their supervisor had already come to a different conclusion. "Yes, you could. But everyone who took part in Kerne's hostage-taking was on TV. She would have seen us all. All of us except…Stacy."

Everyone turned toward the new team member.

Slade's expression was firm, his face hard. "I know it's a big ask. If Lisa Kerne does turn out to be the person we're looking for, she could be extremely dangerous. But as we're—"

"Of course I'll do it." Stacy stared directly at Slade.

Hagen found her agreement unsurprising. She was an FBI agent, after all. He admired her enthusiasm, actually.

Slade took a deep breath. "Good. Now, how do we get you in and do it fast? We don't have time to build you a proper backstory. We're going to have to send you right in."

Stella twisted her gold ear stud, a gift from her father. She often turned it when she was thinking, as though she were winding up her brain and setting the gears in motion. "You said you played the cello, right?"

"Yes, that's right. I'm not world-class or anything. I don't think anyone's going to ask me to fill Carnegie Hall with my solos of Bach's concertos, but—"

"Are you good enough for the Kentwood Philharmonic?" Stella twisted her gold stud faster.

Stacy pondered the question. "The Kentwood Philharmonic? I...I don't know. I was in an orchestra during high school, and I played in a quartet when I was at Penn. We did small events and weddings and so on. But I—"

"Don't shortchange yourself," Mac said, and turned her laptop to face the room. "According to your hometown newspaper, you were a child prodigy."

On the screen was a picture of what appeared to be a ten-year-old Stacy Lark looking tiny next to a cello that probably cost more than most people's cars.

Stacy slapped a hand over her face. "Oh, god. I—"

Slade interrupted this time. "Where are you going with this, Stella?"

"The philharmonic is looking for a new cellist. Lisa Kerne mentioned it when we spoke to her. If Stacy can keep up with the musicians, we'll have a credible way in."

Slade shifted his gaze to Stacy. "What do you think?"

Stacy blew out a long breath. "Well, I had hoped two years with the Philadelphia police and being top of my class at Quantico was going to be more useful in the FBI than my cello-playing abilities. But very well. When's the audition?"

Stella grinned. "They were auditioning today, so we'll try to get you in tomorrow."

"Oh." The agent slid down into her seat. "That's...soon."

24

Stella followed Hagen into Martin's apartment, walking as quietly as she could.

Martin sat in his La-Z-Boy, his hair uncombed and sticking out in all directions. He didn't look up as they came in. His hands lay flat on the arms of the chair. His face was pale and drawn. Dark pouches had settled under his eyes. He looked like he hadn't slept for a month.

Stella stayed at the door, barely entering the room.

Every murder scene, by its nature, contained death. A stiff body. Gray fingers bent by rigor mortis. Eyes open but unseeing, unable to understand why the world moved, but they didn't. Those scenes were still solid. Dead.

This apartment, though, held what death left behind. Grief drifted from Martin's living body like a stench, penetrating the bones. After her father died and again after Jackson's death, Stella breathed that cloying air in her own home.

She had no desire to inhale it once more.

Caleb had gone home to rest, leaving Ander to watch over their friend and coworker.

Ander waved from the kitchen doorway, his phone

pressed to his ear, and the air lightened. There was hope in the presence of a friend, a sign that days could still go on. Stella approached Martin's armchair.

Ander's voice trailed back into the living room.

"Kelsey, listen to me. All I'm saying is, you gotta be careful...no, listen. Jeez. Just keep him at home, will you? ...No...no, I'm not...just for *now*, until I tell you it's okay...I... If you see anything suspicious, anything at all, just call me, okay? ...No, I'm not being..."

Ander's pleas to his ex to keep their son safe intensified. Then Stella no longer heard him over the sound of a running faucet. Tension returned, tightening her chest.

She thought of her mother in Florida, her only living relative. Surely, her mom was far enough away and safe from anything happening here. Stella's stomach clenched at the idea of telling her mom to take care of herself. It would be one more reminder of the dangers of law enforcement.

But she needed to make the call.

Dammit.

She crouched next to the armchair.

Martin turned his watery eyes toward her.

Resting her cast on the coffee table, she took Martin's hand in her free one. "I'm so sorry, Martin. It's just awful. Losing a sibling, it's..."

...one of the worst things in the world. The loss of someone who knows you better than anyone ever will.

A stone had settled at the back of her throat, preventing her from speaking. She waited for a moment, let the stone crumble. "After my brother died...I...I don't think I ever felt so alone. I still speak to him sometimes, you know. I hear his voice. It helps." She ran a thumb over the back of Martin's wrist. "He still makes me laugh too."

Martin kept his gaze on her, but his expression didn't change. He seemed to be somewhere far away, in a place where the murder of his sister hadn't happened, and the pain of this place was absent.

"You're in shock now, I know. That does go away. The pain dulls over time but it's always there. But the shock goes, and you learn to go on."

"Learn to go on?" Martin spoke quietly. The question roused him. "Learn *to go on?*" He withdrew his hand from Stella's and sat up in the chair. "Your brother died of cancer."

Stella swallowed, unsure of Martin's reaction. She couldn't tell whether he was trying to connect or if he was accusing her of something. "Yes. Yes, that's right."

"In a hospital, I'm guessing. Surrounded by doctors and nurses. With morphine to dull the pain and his whole family around him."

The description threw Stella back to the ward. The machine in the corner beeped. A bag next to the bed dripped into a tube that led to Jackson's arm. His chest rose and fell in shallow waves.

Pressure built behind Stella's eyes from the memory. "Yeah. Yeah, we were—"

"Jane died alone." Martin's face reddened. His hand curled into a fist. "In pain. Murdered! By a psycho who cut her *fucking head* off. You've got no *idea* what that's like."

Martin rose and took a stumbling step toward Stella. Hagen intercepted him, holding his shoulder. He didn't try to throw off Hagen's hand, but he glared at Stella, a tear forming in his eye. "There is a big difference, Stella, between losing someone to illness and losing them to a damn killer."

Stella pushed to her feet and stepped back, giving him space. "I understand losing someone violently, too, Martin." The suddenness of the news. The complete, overnight change in a life that she'd just assumed would continue as it always had.

She wanted to yell at Martin that he was wrong, that she

knew far better than he did what was coming. But there was no point. The good days and the bad days would come regardless of what she said now.

Ander appeared in the kitchen doorway, lowering his phone from his ear. "Martin. We know. It's okay. We get it, we—"

Martin spun around. "No, you don't *get it*, Ander. You've never lost anyone. What the hell do *you* know? What are you all doing here, anyway? You should be out there, hunting down the scumbag who did this! You need to bring him in and make sure that bastard gets exactly what he deserves."

Hagen leaned into Martin. It looked like he was providing support, but Hagen had a firm grip on Martin's shoulder. He murmured in his ear. "We are hunting him. We'll find him, Martin. Trust us. We'll find him. And believe me, we will make him pay."

Stella stared at Hagen.

Ander slipped his phone into his pocket and approached Martin. He poured a glass of iced water from the jug on the table and pressed it into Martin's hand.

"Here, drink this." He turned to Hagen and Stella and spoke quietly. "It's okay. I got this. I think you guys should probably, erm…"

Stella agreed with Ander. "We're going to head off now, Martin. We've got some digging to do tonight and an early start tomorrow."

Hagen wrapped a hand around the back of Martin's neck. "Take it easy, okay?"

Neither Stella nor Hagen spoke as they waited for the elevator. Even with the apartment door closed, anger and grief echoed through the corridor like a shock wave, smothering them both.

You don't get it.

That's what Martin had shouted at Ander, and he was

probably right. Ander's family was alive. Healthy. A part of her agreed with Martin. Ander had never survived a violent death. He couldn't get it.

Ping.

The elevator door opened. They stepped inside.

In her heart, she felt what Martin felt. She, too, wanted the killer brought in.

When she searched deep within herself, she also felt the urge to make sure the bastard got what they deserved, to see this madman or woman beaten to a bloody pulp, their limbs smashed, their—

She inhaled sharply.

"You okay?" Hagen didn't look at her, giving her space.

"Sure." It was a lie. The need for vengeance burned, like lifting a hot plate and trying to hold on. It was too much, too strong. Too painful.

And she could see that desire burning in Hagen.

Ping.

The elevator door opened again.

Hagen exited first. He held the street door, waiting for Stella to catch up. "That stuff upstairs getting to you?"

She'd known Hagen less than two months. In that time, they'd cracked no fewer than six cases, had risked their own lives, and saved the lives of others. They'd worked together and trusted each other. They'd confided in each other. She liked him. But only now was Stella starting to feel she understood who he really was. The growing awareness gnawed at her insides. "I'm worried."

"He'll be okay. Like you said, the shock will wear off and he'll learn to live with the grief. As we all do."

"Not about Martin. He'll be fine, especially when we catch his sister's killer. I'm worried about you."

"About me?" Hagen's deep green eyes clouded over, sensing what she was getting at.

She watched as he controlled his expression.

Then the clouds vanished, and he offered a small smile. "I'll be okay. I'm heading down to Amanda's ranch tomorrow. I've told Brianna to meet me there. I'll talk to them about taking precautions and being alert and so on."

"No, that's not—"

Hagen went on, refusing to let her get out what she wanted to say. "You don't worry about me, Stella. I'll look after my family. I always do."

He strode out of the building, leaving Stella by the door. That wasn't what she meant. Not at all. And he knew it.

25

The next morning, sweat dripped from Stella's brow. The Peloton's resistance was too hard for someone with a cracked rib. Her chest screamed.

"Keep going. Burn, burn, burn! You're doing great." The overly intense-yet-perky instructor urged her on from the video screen.

Stella pumped her knees. Each lift of her right leg jolted her ribs. Her thighs ached. But she welcomed the pain. It proved she was alive.

"Aaand relax."

She was free. Her legs slowed to a stop. She lifted her head. The instructor in the Peloton video sat straight on his bike, both thumbs pointed upward, a big grin on his face.

Stella felt like she'd been locked in a sauna for half a day.

This wasn't her usual kind of exercise. She preferred jogging on a trail, earbuds in, and the wind on her cheeks. Trees and sunshine that dappled her face took her out of the city and all its filth.

But the pain from her injury meant running was out.

And the thought of jogging alone through a park, let

alone in the woods by herself, worried her. She wasn't afraid. That wasn't it, not really. If whoever had followed Jane Lin attacked her, she was sure she'd put up a helluva fight, busted rib and broken arm or not. She was even pretty confident she'd win.

But the risk was too stupid to take. If she was going to be bait, she wanted the team behind her, ready to pounce when the killer turned up. Anything else was foolhardy.

The onscreen trainer dropped back onto his handlebars. *"All right, here we go again. Another big hill coming up. Ready? One, two—"*

"Screw that." Stella swiveled off the bike seat.

She stretched her hamstring, resting her heel on the window ledge next to her bag.

On the street, five floors down, all was still. The tops of the gingko trees rolled slightly in the morning breeze, annoyed to be woken so early, and that was it.

Behind her, five Pelotons stood in a neat line, their dark gray crossbars angled like soldiers' weapons on parade. Three of the machines were taken, their riders pedaling fast enough to take the yellow jersey in the Tour de France.

Six thirty on a Saturday morning seemed to be some people's idea of a good time to get hot and tired.

Stella wiped her brow and took a long draught of her water bottle. This certainly wasn't *her* idea of a good time to work out. But she had a feeling she wasn't going to have a spare hour for even a fast walk anytime soon. She had to squeeze in her workouts whenever she could.

She checked her watch. If the time was six thirty in Nashville, it was seven thirty in Florida. Her mom would be up by now. Barbara Knox—now Rotenburg—had always been an early riser, jumping out of bed as dawn broke.

Stella lost count of the number of times she'd come

downstairs to find breakfast made, her lunch packed, and the kitchen cleaned.

She sometimes wondered how her mother did it before reminding herself that her mom was usually in bed by nine p.m. Some people just preferred the mornings.

Stella pulled her phone out of her bag and dialed. Her mother's voice sounded so warm when she answered, so friendly and comforting. "Hey, honey. You're up early."

For a moment, Stella could picture herself back home, curled on the sofa next to her mother, watching *The Price Is Right* together.

"Yeah. Work, you know."

There was silence for a moment. She said four words and managed to make the conversation awkward already.

Stella's mom had never approved of the career Stella had chosen. Losing one family member to criminals was enough. Barbara saw no reason to risk the life of her remaining child in the same way.

And now Stella might just have to tell her she was right.

"Sounds like the FBI is worse than the police department." Her mom's voice remained mild, but Stella heard the small rebuke behind her words. "At least with the police, you knew which shift you were working. And when you were done, you were done."

"Aw, come on, Mom. You know how much overtime Dad used to do. And how often he'd be called out at weird times. There's no nine-to-five in this kind of work."

"Well, yes, honey. That's what I tried to tell you, remember?"

Stella knew too well how hard her mother had tried to persuade her to take a regular job, risking nothing more dangerous than carpal tunnel syndrome from a keyboard.

She changed the subject.

"How's Jonathan?"

Jonathan Rotenberg was Barbara's second husband. He was a retired realtor who had never done anything more adventurous than invest in a Florida condo. His most noteworthy moment was contributing to an Adopt-a-Highway fundraiser.

Their conversations, on the few occasions Stella and Jonathan had them, rarely dipped deeper than polite inquiries before dropping into long silences. But he'd suffered a heart attack recently. The attack wasn't serious, but it had scared Stella's mom.

For some time, Stella had imagined her mother living alone, hundreds of miles away. The thought chilled her.

"Oh, he's much better now, hun. But he won't listen. I keep telling him to take things easy. He shouldn't spend so much time out of doors...*doing stuff*. But you know what he's like. If he doesn't do his eighteen holes every morning or take a walk on the beach at sunset, he thinks he's not really living in Florida."

"Mm." Stella nodded, even though her mom couldn't see her. A round of golf didn't sound particularly tough. A slow drive in a buggy, then a quick swing of a stick before driving on to the next spot.

Stella's dad had worked out five times a week. Keith Knox could carry his two teenage kids, one under each arm.

"I'm sure Jonathan will be fine."

"Well, I hope so."

"And how are you doing?"

"Me? Oh, I'm the same. I've got the Bridge Club coming tonight, so I've got a little shopping to do today. They do like their sandwiches."

"Right. Hey, listen..." Stella wanted to tell her to be careful, warn her against opening the door to strangers. She wanted to give Barbara tips on evading a car tail. She wanted to call local law enforcement and put a guard outside her mother's building. She wanted some beefy officer to shadow Barbara wherever she went.

But the police wouldn't do anything.

Any warning she gave would only frighten her mother.

This killer was in Nashville. No need to scare her mother all the way out in Florida.

The best way to protect her mother was to catch the killer.

The sooner they caught her—if the killer was a her—the better for everyone.

Her mother's voice returned, her concern audible. "What's the matter, honey?"

Last chance.

She shook the thought out of her head.

"Nothing. Nothing. Listen, I gotta go. Enjoy your bridge night and go easy on Jonathan. Don't let him eat too many of your sandwiches. I know what you put in them."

Stella hung up, leaving her mother chuckling. She tossed her phone back into her bag and pulled out a towel. The band of her sports bra was damp with sweat and chafed at her sides. She headed for the changing room.

Her phone rang.

At first, Stella thought her mother might be calling back for some reason.

Reaching the changing room, she sat on the bench and pulled out her phone again. The number was unidentified. A woman in tight shorts and abs like solid brick headed toward the door. Once she left, Stella accepted the call.

"Hello?"

"Stella Knox."

The voice was a man's, deep and slow. The words were a statement, not a question.

"Who is this?"

"You need to be careful, Stella Knox. You're being watched."

Without moving, she scanned the changing room. The benches were empty. No one was in the shower. The door was closed.

Still, she shivered. For the first time since climbing onto the Peloton, she wasn't sweating. A chill settled into her bones.

"Who? Who's watching me?"

"Just be careful, Stella Knox. Be real careful." Raspy breathing created a sound similar to static. Was he running? "And you need to keep an eye on that Hagen Yates. You watch him real close, now."

"Who is this? Who the hell are you?"

"Who am I? Now, let's just say I'm…someone who knew your daddy. Keith Knox, he was a good man. Shouldn't have gone the way he did. No, he should not have. The man who sent him in there, he had no business doing something like that."

Stella was aware she was breathing hard, aware that this strange man's deep voice was right next to her ear. She was aware of nothing else.

"Which man?"

The caller chuckled, then…

The line went dead.

Stella opened her call records and dialed the last number. Her heart raced as she waited to hear the voice again.

A different voice sounded, female and metallic.

"The number you called is not available."

26

Brianna Yates crossed her legs on the sofa and took a slug of cherry coke. She tied her shoulder-length curls into her scrunchie, preparing for some serious studying.

Then she pulled her *Introduction to Medicinal Chemistry* textbook closer.

"I'm going to kick your ass," she told the book.

The house was quiet. All three of Brianna's roommates left last night for the weekend. And in the bright sunlight of Saturday morning, what remained in their wake was…obnoxious.

No one had stopped to clean the place before they'd left. The coffee table was covered in dirty glasses and empty snack wrappers. A fly buzzed over the food-encrusted plates piled in the kitchen sink. Three t-shirts were crumpled on the floor, and a bra hung over the back of a chair behind the kitchen table.

Brianna certainly wasn't going to clean up after any of them—though her righteous stubbornness might give out before the end of the weekend.

But she wasn't going to clean up now. *Time to study.*

Turning to Chapter Nine, she read aloud, "'*Nucleic acids as drug targets.*'"

Taking another long sip, she set the coke on the coffee table, pushing an empty packet of chips out of the way.

Breakfast of champions.

"Ugh. Sounds like the kind of thing Hagen would do. Go nuclear on a drug target."

Tapping the page with the end of a pencil, she started reading. Seconds later, the letters began to swim. Her eyes skipped words. She missed the meaning of a sentence, misunderstood the next, and shook her head.

Focus! You don't have that long before the exam.

She checked the clock on the wall above the sofa.

The plain white face and black rim hung at an angle. The eleven pointed almost straight up, and the twelve was where the one should be. A pillow fight in February was responsible for the tilt.

Molly, one of Brianna's housemates, had lobbed a cushion at her, which Brianna had deflected, knocking the clock to one side. No one had gotten around to adjusting the face, so they'd all grown used to checking the time with their heads cocked to the right.

"Seven already. Shit."

In a couple of hours, she'd have to leave for her sister's place. She probably shouldn't have promised to go riding with Amanda before their late lunch, especially since it took nearly three hours to get to her ranch. But her sister had been so adamant that refusal felt like an insult.

And the thought of a ride through the country did bring Brianna a little thrill of anticipation.

First, though, she had to study.

Although the semester had only recently ended, she needed the credits from a summer class to get into medical school. However hard this stuff was to remember.

Sometimes, she wondered if she should've gone into law enforcement like her brother. Legal jargon would certainly have been easier to study than nucleic acids and the density of molecules. But there'd been enough law-and-order workers in the family.

And she didn't want to be like her father. For Seth Yates, the law seemed to have been mostly about loopholes, arguments, and hourly rates broken into fifteen-minute periods.

She wanted a career where success wasn't measured by a bank statement. Work that was meaningful and made a difference. She wanted to save people and make their lives better.

Hagen did that, in his own way.

Chasing criminals down and arresting them so they didn't harm others. She admired what he did, but she knew that kind of action wasn't for her. She wanted face-to-face contact, bringing help to one person at a time. Brianna wanted to see the results of her effort.

"Topoisomerase poisons. Non-intercalating." She rolled her eyes. "Well, of course, *non*-intercalating. You wouldn't want the *intercalating* topographic…topo-something-or-other poisons, would you? Silly."

Not much of this stuff made sense. Certainly not much was sticking in her brain.

But the more she studied, the more she'd remember.

She bent lower over the textbook, talking to herself. "Focus."

Bam. Bam. Bam.

The knock on the door jarred her. Hard like a cop's knock.

Ba-bam. Bam. Bam.

Brianna got up and peered through the blinds.

A young woman stood on the doorstep. She wore torn black jeans and a black tank top. A tote bag decorated with a large white rabbit dangled from her shoulder. Her hair was loose and reached to her shoulders. A thick strand stuck to her face where blood ran down her cheek from her temple.

"Jeez."

Judging by the strength with which the woman was banging on the door, her health wasn't in any immediate danger. But she could be in shock, and if she had a wound, it would need cleaning and patching.

Brianna could handle that.

She unlocked the door. The woman was halfway into the house before Brianna had even finished opening it.

"Oh, thank you. You've got to help me. Please! It's awful. I…there's been an accident. A dog. I was just driving down the road when a dog…a big dog, like a…I don't know…a Dobermann or something? It just ran into the road right in front of me. I…I had to swerve. There was a…a tree…and oh, my gosh."

She touched her temple and stared at the blood on her fingers.

Brianna gripped the woman's shoulders, trying to steady her. The woman was slim and bony. Brianna felt her scapula under her skin. She'd just been reading about shoulder bones in an anatomy class.

She led the stranger to the sofa and sat her down.

The woman put her hand to her temple and closed her eyes.

"No, no. Don't lie down. You have to stay awake. You might have a concussion."

"Oh. I'm feeling a little…a little strange."

"It's just shock. I've got a first aid kit in the bathroom. I'll go get it."

Brianna took two steps away from the sofa then paused, something striking her as odd about the situation. The crash must have been big to draw that much blood.

But she'd heard nothing, even though the street was empty, and the house was quiet. Brianna started to turn. "Where did you say—"

She didn't finish her sentence. A blow struck her on the right side of her skull. A sickening flash of golden-orange light passed through her head just before the room turned dark.

27

I knew I'd need a good couple of hours to get from Brianna Yates's house to north of Nashville. The drive back to the school was long. That's why I'd set out so good and early.

Brianna fit neatly in my trunk—she was smaller than Jane Lin. Besides, if she recovered on the way, I didn't want her screaming and banging on the windows for help, all terrified and bloody-faced.

But she was dead quiet so far. And that was fine by me.

I tuned to a classical station as I drove, trying not to think about the FBI agents or Jane Lin or anything but the present and future.

There was a game I liked to play. It was one my dad had taught me.

First, I'd try to see how many notes I needed to identify a piece of music.

Beethoven's Piano Sonata no. 14 in C-sharp Minor. Got that one in the first bar.

Then, I'd listen to the piano part—if there was one—and list all the ways I'd have played that piece better. When my father was alive, I'd say my list aloud. Now, I offered commentary.

"Come on, man. Give it a bit of passion. Let the note linger a little. There's emotion in that composition. You're killing it. And not in the good way."

As I drove over the bridge spanning the Tennessee River, the music stopped, and the news came on.

"A body was found in the basement of the old Merys High School. The victim, a woman from New York down to visit her brother. The killing, brutal and sadistic."

My blood ran as cold as the brown water beneath me, and I pulled onto the hard shoulder. A truck roared past, its horn blowing.

"What the actual hell?!"

Desperately needing fresh air, I hopped out of the car, slamming the door.

I paced along the side of the bridge, forcing myself to calm down. I'd done so well in front of the agents. I couldn't lose my shit now.

"Don't lose your shit now, Lisa!"

That was always the big difference between my father and me. He was always so meticulous, so precise. He thought and he planned and he practiced until he had everything exactly the way he wanted. I always went on instinct and let my emotions rule me.

And Hagen Yates had truly pissed me off.

In response, instead of planning what to do next, what did I do instead? Take off like a maniac and abduct his damn sister.

Now here I was, standing alone by a river, with a Fed's sister unconscious or dead in the trunk of my car…and I was on my way to the damn school where they'd discovered Lin's body. And head. "Stupid, stupid, stupid!"

The school was crawling with cops. Of course it was. "Stupid!"

Where do I take her now?

"Where?!"

And my father was dead. There was no one to ask for help or even advice.

The water churned beneath me. Its current was strong and sure. I could get rid of Brianna Yates now. Wait until the bridge was empty, then drag her out of the trunk and just drop her clean over the side.

She'd probably be dead as soon as she hit the water, if she wasn't already.

An SUV shot past on the other side of the road. The driver watched me from under his baseball cap as he drove. Probably wondering whether I needed help. A woman stuck on the side of a bridge. That was a real temptation for some men.

"Why, yes, sir. I sure could do with some assistance. Thank you. You take the legs. I'll take the head. And one, two, three…*kersplash*. Why, sir, you're a real gent."

I sounded like a lunatic.

The river wouldn't work. I'd probably be seen throwing her in.

And then I'd miss all the fun of keeping her around and finishing her off at my leisure. Being fished out of a river like some old piece of driftwood just wasn't what I had in mind for Hagen Yates's sister.

He was the triggerman—the one who actually shot my dad.

I wanted him to suffer.

He needed to understand what it was like to miss someone he loved.

He needed to feel the pain and all the emptiness that followed.

Another truck came up behind me, slowing down. I pulled out my phone and pretended to take a picture, like I was some kind of tourist overwhelmed by the sight of a wide expanse of dirty water.

The truck passed on. I climbed back into the car and drove.

"Where to go? Where to go?"

My house was too small. There was nowhere to hide her there and no way to keep her from escaping. And besides, getting the blood off the walls would be murder if I used my now-trusty axe, sitting there in my bag.

The opening bars of Beethoven's Fifth. Got it in one note.

Then I realized it was my ringtone.

Ugh, just leave me alone.

But I answered.

"Lisa, darling. I have a huuuge favor to ask of you."

Amy Cooper, the director of the Kentwood Philharmonic. I tried to avoid her as much as I could. She could be so smarmy, so subservient to the donors. Amy always knew what buttons to push to open cash registers.

I tried to keep the irritation out of my voice as I answered. "I have the morning off, Amy, and I'm—"

"The thing is, the accompanist has called in sick. We have auditions for the new third cello lined up all afternoon. If you could come in right away, I would be *so* grateful."

The request didn't even anger me. I just brushed it off. "Like I said, I have the morning off, and I do have plans, so I'm afraid—"

"The thing is, Lisa, your contract stipulates I can call you in at any time to help with such things as private events, publicity…and auditions. So strictly speaking, *not* turning up would be a breach of contract. And I'm sure you wouldn't want to break your contract, would you?"

Anger began to boil inside me. I almost told her where

she could stick her contract, and I was in a pretty good mind to put it there myself next time I saw her. It was a shame Amy wasn't related to an FBI agent.

But then I remembered.

In the basement of the philharmonic was a rehearsal room everyone seemed to have forgotten about. Sometimes, I sat down there, deep in the earth, and tried to forget the world. It had been built for percussionists.

The soundproofing was excellent.

"You know what, you're right. What time are you expecting everyone today?"

"Oh, that's wonderful. I knew I could count on you. People are already arriving. It's all such a mess."

"I'll be there as soon as I can."

I hit the gas.

28

Hagen tapped the steering wheel of his Corvette and checked his watch. The timepiece was his father's, a 1974 Patek Phillippe Calatrava with a white dial and simple gold case that masked its five-figure value.

He'd only pulled into the parking lot behind the Kentwood Philharmonic a few minutes ago, but already he was keen to leave.

He'd agreed to drive down to Amanda's ranch that afternoon for a late lunch around two with both sisters, a rare treat he hadn't managed for months. But the philharmonic had phoned Stacy an hour earlier. The accompanist was sick, and they were running late while they looked for another. *"Could you come in a little later?"*

Of course she could.

And, of course, that meant Hagen was running late for lunch with his sisters.

A dark blue Ford Explorer pulled into the lot and parked next to Hagen. Stacy climbed out of the driver's side and slipped into the Corvette's passenger seat. Her face was set, but a thin layer of perspiration disturbed the foundation on her forehead.

Hagen turned up the air-conditioning. He needed her calm, cool, and collected. "Let's talk fast. Risky sitting here in the parking lot. You good?"

Stacy folded her hands in her lap, always prim. "A little nervous."

"First time undercover?"

"Oh, no, it's not the undercover work. I'm not infiltrating a crime gang or anything. Just trying to get close to one person. I'm sure I can handle that." She swallowed. "It's the audition. I haven't auditioned since I was a sophomore in college. The thought scares the living daylights out of me. Frankly, I'd rather go head to head with an axe-wielding serial killer than face a bank of audition judges again."

"Well, you may have to do both." Hagen offered her a sardonic smile. "We can lean on the philharmonic's director to get you in if we really have to. But we'd rather not. The fewer people who know who you are and what we're doing, the better."

Stacy gave a small nod. She pulled a tissue out of her clutch and dabbed her forehead.

A young woman strode from the corner of the parking lot. She was shorter than Stacy but she, too, wore a knee-length black skirt and white shirt. Her hair was pulled back into a neat ponytail.

The woman noticed the Corvette and its occupants. She approached and tapped on the window.

"Y'all here for the audition?"

Stacy lowered the window. "I am."

The woman eyed Hagen and gave him a little wink. "Shame it's just you. Well, you can take your time. They're still running late. The pianist *still* hasn't gotten here. Could be a while, they said. But, get this, it's *the* Lisa Kerne."

Hagen and Stacy exchanged a quick glance. *Looks like Stacy's going to be getting really close, really soon.*

The woman took a hit off her vape. The vanilla-scented steam drifted into the car. "You want to come and wait inside with us, you're more than welcome. Entrance is around the front. This door here is only for people who are already staff."

"Sounds great. I'll be there in a second."

The woman tapped the top of the car, then made her way to the entrance of the philharmonic building.

Hagen's phone rang. Amanda's name lit up on the screen. He glanced at Stacy. "My sister. I should take it."

"I'll go get my cello."

As Stacy left the Corvette and retrieved her instrument from the trunk of her Explorer, Hagen took the call. His sister's voice was so warm and familiar after Stacy's tight nerves and upper-class lilt. Hagen relaxed.

"Hey, Amanda. How's it going?"

"Just great. Clint's brushing down the horses, and I'm busy chopping the salad. And you're not here."

"Yeah, listen. I'm gonna be a little late, but I'll—"

"You too? Aw, Hagen. If you and Brianna let my meatloaf dry out, I will not be happy."

Hagen frowned. "Brianna's not there yet?"

"Nope. And she was supposed to be here an hour ago. Said she was gonna ride Marybelle with me before lunch. But she's not here and she's not answering her phone. Typical. I'm telling you, she is so darned inconsiderate. We all have to adjust ourselves to whatever she feels like doing whenever she feels like doing it. She can be such a *flake* sometimes."

Hagen didn't hear the singsong tone of her complaint. He'd stopped listening after hearing Brianna wasn't answering her phone. His chest tightened and his fingers trembled on the steering wheel.

"I'll call her."

He hung up and called. The phone rang and rang again, then switched to voicemail.

"You've reached Brianna Yates. I'm not able to take your call—"

Hagen rolled down the window of the passenger seat and called to Stacy. "I need to go. Call me when you're done."

He opened the throttle, not waiting for Stacy to answer.

29

Hagen pushed his foot to the floor. The Corvette growled and the wheels clattered over the Jimmy Evans Memorial Bridge. The trip from Kentwood to Bethel University usually took roughly two and a half hours. He'd been on the road for almost ninety minutes and was nearly there.

Just let some traffic cop try to stop me.

The speedometer ticked up.

Eighty miles an hour.

Ninety.

A hundred.

He roared past a truck and shot toward the back of an SUV clinging to the speed limit in the passing lane. He flashed his lights and sounded his horn. The SUV puttered on. Hagen slid to the right and overtook on the inside, cutting back on the left close enough to attract a loud honk from the SUV's driver. He soon left the car far behind.

He had to get there.

She was his responsibility, his little sister. It was up to him to make sure she was safe and well and provided for.

Since his father had gone, that had always been his job.

He could call the local police and have them do a wellness check, he knew. He probably should, but dammit...he needed to do this himself.

"Call Brianna," he told his phone.

Straight to voicemail now. Her battery might be dead.

"You've reached Brianna Yates. I'm not able to take your call—"

Her voice roared through the car speakers.

Brianna...

She was such a sweet kid. Amanda was right—Brianna could be disorganized and forgetful, but she was also kind and considerate, and no one was more generous.

After their father's murder, he'd found her sitting on the swing in the backyard. She was just seven years old but had a faraway look in her eyes, like an old woman who'd seen too much.

Brianna didn't answer when he asked what she was doing. He knew. Some things just didn't need to be said.

So he'd stood behind her and pushed. Up she swung, laughing for the first time since the funeral. For an hour, he pushed her without complaining. At last, when Brianna climbed off the swing, her legs wobbly and thoughts of her lost dad pushed to a distance, she insisted Hagen take her place.

"It's your turn now."

"But you can't push me. I'm too big."

She thought for a moment, then ran halfway back to the house, calling for Amanda at the top of her voice. When her sister came running out, she explained they needed to push Hagen on the swing.

"He pushed me. Now we'll push him. Then we'll push you. We'll do everything together."

"Everything together," he murmured to himself, slamming the gas pedal to the floor.

His phone rang. Without glancing at the screen, he jammed the answer button on the steering wheel.

"Brianna?"

"Er, sorry. No. Stacy." Hagen's heart sank. "Just wanted to let you know it looks like I got the job."

The job? Of course, the job.

"Really? That's great. Really great." He hoped he sounded normal.

"They said they'd be in touch with a contract. But they mentioned they were very impressed. They thought I'd fit right in, and they wanted to know if I was available for rehearsal this afternoon. There's some sort of charity performance tonight. Of course, I told them I was."

"Good. That's great. Tell Slade, will you?"

"Sure." The line became silent for a moment, then Stacy continued. "There was one thing."

Hagen smothered a spark of irritation. "What's that?"

"The pianist. It *was* Lisa Kerne."

"Did you speak to her?"

"No. She turned up about forty minutes after you left. She didn't speak to anyone. I thought she looked a bit out of sorts, like something was on her mind. She took my score and started playing. She made a couple of mistakes, small ones, but she was really very good. She's quite a talent. As soon as I finished, she left without a word."

"Okay, good. The audition will give you something to talk about when you meet." Hagen pulled off the highway. The student houses weren't far from the main road.

He started to speak, then hesitated. He didn't want to raise an alarm unnecessarily.

But as more time passed without word from Brianna, the more worried he became. The team should know.

"Listen. My sister's not answering her calls. I'm checking on her right now."

"Oh, heavens. It's probably just—"

"Yeah, probably. I just...I need to check. I'll let you know what I find. Don't forget to update Slade."

He shut off the call.

Ten minutes later, he pulled up outside Brianna's house.

The place looked quiet enough. The blinds were down, though the last slats on the right had bent up at an angle. A Bethel University pennant was hung across the top of the glass. A line of beer bottles stood in one of the upstairs windows, boldly declaring to the world that the bedroom's resident knew how to party.

Brianna's Honda Civic was the only car in the driveway.

Hagen took the porch steps in one stride and jammed his finger into the doorbell. The buzz sounded through the house as though a swarm of bees had taken over the living room.

No one answered.

Hagen put his hand over the windowpane and tried to peer through the bent slats. He couldn't see much, just enough to note the living room was a mess, as always. Snack wrappers littered the coffee table. Two empty glasses stood upright. A third had fallen over.

Students.

He was glad that part of his life was far behind him.

Hagen took his phone from his pocket and called again.

"You've reached Brianna Yates. I'm not able to take your call—"

This time, he left a message. "Brianna, you better call me back right now."

He paced to the end of the porch and rested the small of his back against the rail.

And that was when he saw it. Next to the doormat, about an inch from the wall, was a single red splotch. The mark was about the size of a quarter, the edges forming an uneven crown.

Hagen didn't move. He knew he should.

The half-dried stain sucked all his attention.

A checklist of things that needed to happen next ran through his mind.

He needed to secure the scene. He needed to contact the local authorities and Slade. He needed to do a sweep of the exterior.

A forensic scientist would scrape a sample for DNA testing.

But he couldn't do any of these things yet.

If he didn't move, he wouldn't know, not for certain.

He'd still have hope.

The color was as dark and rich as every splash of blood he'd ever seen. Maybe the same color as Jane Lin's in the basement of Merys High School.

There were no other marks or any sign of forced entry on the door.

The single bloodstain alone was enough.

Hagen drew his foot back and was about to kick the door in when his phone rang. Slade.

He didn't bother with a hello. "Sir, I'm going in."

"No, you're not. We're doing this by the book. The locals are on the way."

As if on cue, the wail of sirens rose from the distance.

"But, sir—"

"Hagen! Listen to me, dammit. You are not going inside your sister's house. That's an order."

As police cars screamed to a stop in front of Brianna's little house, Hagen sank to the porch. He knew why Slade didn't want him inside.

He doesn't want me to be the one to find my little sister's head...

30

Stella paced the hallway of the enormous medical office building. Mac was in one of the treatment rooms, receiving a final checkup to assess her healing process after being abducted and tortured only twelve days ago.

She didn't want to disturb her friend, but Stella really needed to speak to Mac. She jammed her thumbs into the pockets of her slacks and continued her pacing.

Stella only arrived five minutes ago, but each minute felt like an hour. Her shoes squeaked against the linoleum floor. A middle-aged man stretched a leg into Stella's path and probed the back of his knee with his fingers.

Two nurses emerged from a room marked *Orthopedics* and headed in Stella's direction. One clutched a clipboard to her chest. Laughing, she declared, "I would've just *died* if that had happened to me."

Stella stepped aside to let them pass, wondering only briefly what had happened.

The middle-aged man with the lame leg ignored both Stella and the nurses. Wincing, he pushed harder into the back of his knee, as though a little extra pressure would fix everything.

As Stella reached the middle of the hallway, the door of the treatment room opened, and Mac emerged at last. Instead of a bandage, a thin pink line crossed her temple and slipped under the hairline above her ear. The ragged cut was now clean and looked like it would barely scar.

Mac was fixed, at least on the outside. Stella felt a small pang of jealousy. The last of the dressings were long gone and the mark that remained would fade eventually. Stella ran her fingers absent-mindedly along her cast.

Her friend half-skipped toward her. "Hey, Stella. You didn't have to wait for me here."

She touched Stella's upper arm. For a moment, Stella assumed Mac was trying to help *her*.

But she quickly realized Mac was trying to steady herself. The smile that came so easily to Mac's face was missing. Removing the wound dressing and seeing the new scar must've reminded Mac of her abduction and torture, including waterboarding. That wasn't a memory anyone would want to recall.

The moment didn't last. Having physical contact with a friend must have calmed Mac down. In a second, her familiar grin was back. She pulled Stella's one good arm into her own and led her toward the exit.

"What was so urgent you had to drive all the way out here to see me?"

Stella kept her voice low. "Not here."

She led Mac past the elevators and onto a garden terrace that ran around the building. She listened carefully. Only when she was satisfied that the place was empty, with no patients sneaking out for a quiet cigarette behind the juniper bush, did Stella guide Mac to a corner.

"I got a call this morning."

"Hope it was the lottery. Remember your friends."

Usually, she was grateful for Mac's moments of levity. But she still heard that deep voice at the end of the line and recalled the warning. She was wound too tight to smile.

Mac sensed Stella's tension. She drew closer, lowering her voice. "Sorry. What was it? What happened?"

"Some guy. The number was unidentified. He said he knew my dad."

"Wow. What did he want?"

"He said someone was watching me."

"Jeez, Stella." Mac glanced past the potted plants on the terrace, then stood on her toes to peer over the parapet at the parking lot below. The absence of any obvious spy seemed to satisfy her, and she dropped back onto her feet. "Have *you* noticed anything?"

"Not a thing. If he's telling the truth, whoever's following me is a lot better than the last guy."

"That sounds scary as hell."

"He said my dad shouldn't have died, that…that…" Stella's voice caught, a wave of emotion hitting her harder than she'd expected. She swallowed and pushed on. "That the man who did it had no business killing him."

Mac put a hand on Stella's shoulder. "Sounds like we got a mystery helper. He give a reason for being so nice?"

"No. And there was something else."

"What's that?"

"He told me to watch out for Hagen. Sounded kinda scared of him."

Mac lowered her hand. She drew back, staring at Stella. "Hm. Maybe this guy isn't so helpful after all. He's probably just playing with you, trying to drive the team apart. And anyway, what would he know about Hagen?"

"I don't know. But I do worry about Hagen. Sometimes, I

think when we get to the bottom of this, he's going to...I don't know. Go off the rails or something."

"I...look, Hagen can be..." Mac breathed out slowly, looking for the right words. "He can be determined. And hard to stop once he gets going. But he's also a professional. He knows what he's doing. I don't think you should listen to your mystery caller. Not about Hagen. You don't know what his agenda is."

A surge of relief shot through Stella. Mac was right. Listening to an anonymous caller wasn't the wisest decision. This situation needed caution and careful thinking. "Do you think you can track the call? I tried calling back, but the line was unavailable. Is there anything you can do? Whoever that guy was, he could turn out to be even more helpful than Uncle Joel."

Mac, always up for a tech challenge, smiled. "Yeah. I mean, it won't be easy. But I'll see what I can do."

"Thanks, Mac."

Stella closed her eyes and took a deep breath to steady her nerves. When she opened them again, she found Mac looking at her quizzically.

"Sorry. It just feels like we're getting somewhere, you know? I feel jittery. Like after all this time, I'm reaching the end of a tunnel. The walls are getting tight, and the hole is pretty small, but if I can keep going, the way through is dead ahead. But I've been in the tunnel so long, I'm not sure what to expect on the other side. Nerve-wracking and exciting at the same time."

Mac fixed her eyes on her friend, serious now. "Yeah. Just don't get dead trying to squeeze your way out."

The hair on Stella's arms rose. "I'll be okay. Let's get back into the office, see if—"

She was interrupted by her phone. The sound made her

freeze, but she shook it off almost immediately. Not every caller would be her so-called informant.

"It's Slade." Then Stella answered the call. "Hey, Boss."

"Stella, listen up." Slade's voice was low and tight, as though it had been pushed too far and pulled too long. "Brianna Yates, Hagen's sister, is missing."

Her stomach tightened so much it hurt. "When?"

Mac leaned in, listening. Stella was grateful for her warmth.

"Since this morning. She didn't turn up at her sister's, and she hasn't answered her phone. Hagen's at her place now. He thinks he's found blood by the door. I'm on my way there."

Stella leaned into Mac, if only to feel someone solid next to her.

"What do you want me to do?"

"Where are you?"

"At the doctor's office with Mac."

Slade paused. Stella could almost hear his brain working. "Good. Tell Mac to go to the office. She needs to contact Special Agent Chan and follow up on Anne Lawson. I'll send Chloe and Caleb out to Lawson's residence. You meet Ander in Kentwood, and you two see if Lisa Kerne knows anything. Get alibis. Hagen and I will look for more physical evidence."

31

Hagen sat on the curb outside Brianna's house, elbows on his knees. Just yesterday he'd been sitting on the street outside Merys High School with Stella, trying to wrap his head around the blood and body parts he'd seen.

There was much less blood here. A single drop by the door. But as far as he was concerned, that drop might as well have been a lake's worth.

At least Brianna wasn't inside.

Forensics was already in the house. A line of yellow tape flapped in the early afternoon breeze. Someone in a white suit strode past him to place another bag into the back of a van.

They didn't stop to reassure him, to ask how he was doing. What had been his sister's student housing, a place of youth and fun and far too many discarded food packets and unwashed clothes, was now a crime scene. And he was no longer an FBI agent...he was a family member. His credentials no longer mattered.

Footsteps sounded behind him, solid and heavy.

Slade took a seat on the curb next to him. A chopper had gotten him to the scene in record time.

Hagen immediately pressed him. "What have they found in there?"

Slade seemed comfortable on the sidewalk. In fact, Hagen had never seen his supervisor look uncomfortable in any situation. He would squat beside a small child to be less intimidating or stand for hours in a command center, guiding teams, without seeming fatigued.

"That spot of blood you saw by the door? The HemaTrace indicates it's not blood at all. They think it's more likely to be food coloring or stage blood or something."

Confusion washed over Hagen like a tsunami, smashing away the dark sickness that had roiled in his stomach for a couple hours now.

But there was no relief.

"I'm sorry. I really thought…when I saw the blood, or whatever it is, and remembered what happened to Martin's sister…I just thought the worst."

Slade's serious expression didn't change. Somehow, that made Hagen genuinely scared.

"The cases *are* connected. Whoever took Brianna also wrote *Chop, chop, FBI* on the television screen. Used a permanent marker."

"What?"

"While the spot outside the door isn't blood, forensics found traces of blood on the sofa and by the door. Brianna isn't with any of her housemates or in class. We've checked. We found her phone inside. It had fallen under the table."

The sickness returned, a black hole in Hagen's guts. Brianna wouldn't even take out the garbage without her phone.

Brianna, where the hell are you?

Hagen wanted to scream but found for the first time that

he had no energy. He couldn't move, couldn't even bring himself to stand. If he made even the slightest shift, all the pain of Brianna's disappearance would collapse on top of him, burying him under a ton of guilt and regret.

He should have done more. He should have protected her. It was his job.

He remembered the day his father had died. Brianna... she'd just looked so confused. She'd carried on with her dolls' tea party, asking when Daddy would be coming back. And Hagen didn't know what to say or what to do or how to tell her. He'd sat down with her, letting her pour imaginary tea while they ate a whole box of Oreos. Their mother hadn't stopped them.

He'd never felt so helpless.

Until now.

Slade pushed to his feet. "Hagen, we're going to find her. Trust us. We *will* find her. I promise."

Promises weren't worth the breath it took to make them, Hagen knew. He wanted action. He wanted his sister back, and he wanted her *now*.

"It's Lisa Kerne, isn't it? She's got her."

Slade's jaw set, as if he was preparing to physically stop Hagen if he tried something stupid. "We don't know that. There's no reason to believe she does. Stacy's at the philharmonic, watching her like a hawk. I've sent Stella and Ander to talk to her."

"Then the neighbor. The woman next to the school. The strange one with the piles of chopped-up wood and booze and a missing husband."

"Chloe and Caleb are speaking to her. I just spoke to Chloe. She says Lawson was home alone all last night and—"

"No alibi! Again."

"Easy. We don't have a strong motive. Her husband leaving her for an Asian FBI agent is...*shaky* at best. And

Chloe and Caleb are still there. The woman's given them access to the house. Chloe says there's no obvious place she could have hidden anyone. They're going to do a thorough walk-through of the high school, too, since they're already there. But if you want my personal opinion…my *gut*…is that Lisa Kerne is more likely our killer. I agree with Stella. She's got good instincts."

Hagen shot to his feet. Slade lifted a hand, cutting off whatever he was going to say and stopping him cold. "Listen, I need *you* to do something. The team is focused on the two suspects we've got. I've put out a BOLO. The police and highway patrol are looking for Brianna. They're turning over every rock and following every lead. I've also asked for officers to help guard family members, but I want you to go to your sister's ranch and stay there. I'll have someone escort you. I'm relying on you to help protect Amanda. Do you understand?"

Hagen bit back a sharp reply. He understood. He got it perfectly. Slade didn't want him going off on his own. His supervisor was trying to handle him the way he handled Martin. Slade knew what Hagen would do if he got to Lisa or Anne before the rest of the team did.

And Slade had found the one thing that might just hold him in place.

"Okay."

Slade patted him on the shoulder. "Good. There's nothing for you to do here. Now go make sure that ranch is secure. Your other sister's depending on you."

32

At the Kentwood Philharmonic, the rising notes of the orchestra drifted out of the auditorium, filling the foyer with a warm, welcoming tone.

Walking in, Stella noticed the benefit concert was in honor of the late Jeremy Deem, a man who had given a great deal of funding to the orchestra. He'd been murdered, along with his wife and mother-in-law, by Boris Kerne.

"They're having Lisa Kerne play in a memorial concert for a man her father *murdered*?" Stella arched an eyebrow at Ander. "That certainly falls under the heading of 'stressor.'"

Stressors were often keys to a killer's actions. Divorce, job loss, and death of loved ones were huge predictors of violent behavior. People who were not emotionally equipped to deal with the pressure could lash out.

Ander seemed doubtful. "Yeah, but do you think it would turn her into an axe murderer? Wouldn't she just...quit?"

"Well, she hasn't quit."

"I wonder how Jeremy Deem's family feels about that. Not the most sensitive move in the world, is it?"

"His son Jem might think it's poetic justice."

In a few hours, wealthy donors would arrive in their suits and their jewels to hear some Bach and Beethoven and Schumann and write big checks to honor one of the philharmonic's most generous donors.

While Ander pulled the door closed behind her, Stella examined a poster. A thin beam from an unseen spotlight glowed on a piano keyboard. The name of the orchestra was emblazoned at the top of the sheet above Jeremy Deem's name. There was no mention of the names of the conductor or any of the soloists.

"But who knows? Maybe the Deem family wanted Lisa's participation to show they don't blame her. Her father was the killer, after all, not her. And he got the justice he deserved. Or as close to justice as we could give him."

Ander tilted his head, as though a new physical angle would let him see the benefit concert in a new way. "I dunno. I still think the orchestra should have asked her to sit this one out. I don't think I want to be around the kid of someone who killed my old man. Probably Amy Cooper, milking it for headlines and funds. She seems the type."

Stella didn't agree with Ander. She had no problem forgiving the daughter of the man who'd ordered her father's death. If she wasn't involved herself. And as long as the woman's father got the justice he deserved, she could separate the family from the killer.

She pulled open the door of the auditorium and started down the stairs.

The stage was full. The conductor stood at the podium, his baton in his hand, his long white hair swinging past his ears. The horns held their brass instruments at the ready. Violinists gently stroked their instruments, their elbows held up like servers carrying overladen trays.

Lisa Kerne sat hunched over the piano, her thin arms as

white as the ivory keys. And there were the cellists, three of them, sitting at the back, their eyes fixed on the score.

Stacy looked so different here. Her forehead was creased in concentration. Her fingers danced over the strings at the top of her instrument. She made the performance look so natural. The undercover agent barely had to move, and her instrument resonated throughout the hall. A flick of her fingers, a shift of her wrist, and it was done.

Envy gave Stella a bitter taste at the back of her throat. Everything she accomplished required deferred satisfaction.

She'd investigate for days, weeks, even years, hoping that eventually, one day, she'd get the reward she wanted. At some point in the future, she'd find another scrap of evidence or discover a new lead. Over time, she would put the pieces together and, gradually, a picture would emerge. The process took so long and demanded so much effort.

Stacy had only to press a string and pull her bow, and out came a perfect note, a perfect piece of music. How satisfying that must be. How unlike law enforcement. Given her clear talent, Stella wondered what drew the woman to a career so opposite from one in music.

As if hearing her thoughts, Stacy looked up, but her expression didn't change. She turned the page of her score.

Dung.

The piano made a ringing, discordant noise.

"For fuck's sake!" Lisa dropped her hands from the keyboard and turned to the rest of the orchestra.

The singing of the violins drifted away. The cellos stopped their growling.

Everyone stared at Lisa.

Lisa, however, was defiant. "Yeah, I made a mistake. Whaddya know? It's almost like I'm human."

The conductor lowered his baton. "Lisa, that's the third time today."

"You think I don't know? I..." Her gaze landed on Stella standing halfway down the stairs, then on Ander. "Not you two again." Real fury laced her words.

"She does seem stressed," Ander muttered in Stella's ear. "I think she'd definitely kill us."

"And our families."

The conductor glared at the intruders, seeming just as angry and stressed as Lisa. "I'm sorry, but we're in the middle of a rehearsal. I don't know who you think you are, but you can't just come waltzing into the auditorium anytime you—"

"We're FBI." Stella held up her ID. "But you're right. I can't speak for my colleague here, but I can't waltz, like, at all. I do need to speak to your pianist for a few minutes, though."

The conductor's shoulders fell. He tapped the top of his music stand. "Okay, let's take ten, everyone. I think we all need a break anyway."

Lisa's hands landed on her hips. "Now, wait just a second. I think we need to keep going. We've got a lot to get through before tonight."

But the cellists were already setting down their instruments and the violinists were placing their bows across their chairs.

The conductor strode toward the stairs at the wings of the stage, following a couple of trumpeters keen to give their lips a rest. "And we all need a break, Lisa. Especially you."

One of the cellists followed the conductor, but the second leaned back in her seat and pulled out her phone. Stacy copied her new comrade, stretching her long legs past her instrument. She still didn't look in the direction of Stella and Ander, but somehow Stella was grateful for her presence.

Lisa remained on her piano stool. A paper cup sat on the floor next to her, and she picked it up and sipped.

"I'd offer you some tea, but the kettle's backstage. And you might actually stick around to drink it."

Ander dragged a couple of chairs over. He pushed one toward Stella and sat in the other. "You're making me think you don't want us here."

"I don't." Lisa trapped the string of the tea bag under her finger and sipped again. "Don't take it personally. We've got a performance tonight and a rehearsal to get through."

Stella turned the chair around and sat with her legs spread and her casted arm resting on the back of the seat. "Where were you last night, Lisa?"

Lisa shrugged. "Here. Playing. Same as always. Musicians like me, we don't have much of a life."

Ander leaned forward in his seat. The chairs were cheap and plastic, the kind that lost their comfort within seconds. "You think we do?"

Lisa sized him up. A small smile bent her lips. "You? No."

"And where were you this morning?"

Lisa sipped her tea again. She thought before she answered. "Hmm, let's see. Oh, yeah. Got a call to come in and help out with an audition. We got ourselves a new cellist. All bright and shiny."

She lifted her tea toward the cellists on the other side of the stage.

Stacy looked up. She smiled and waved to Lisa, who raised her cup higher in acknowledgment. "See, she needs the practice. Not even leaving for a break."

Stella turned back to Lisa. "What time was that?"

"The audition? I don't know. Got the call around nine thirty or so. I was out for a drive. Wanted to get some air in my lungs before I spent the afternoon in this hall. If I'd known I was going to have to spend the morning in here as well, I'd have left earlier."

"Where did you go?"

"Nowhere special. Out past the Jimmy Evans bridge. Seeing the water helps sometimes, you know? You should try it. Might help to wash away some of that tension in your shoulders. Lucky you're not a pianist. Can't play with that kind of stress."

She looked Stella up and down, as though she were measuring her for a fitting.

Stella was unconcerned by Lisa's examination. "Maybe you should have spent more time on the bridge. Looked like you were having some difficulty with that last piece. Maybe I'm not the one under stress?"

Lisa's expression was ice cold. "Just out of form. Nothing a little practice won't fix."

Stella pulled out her phone. Looking at the screen, she directed another question at Lisa. "You drove alone this morning?"

"Uh-huh. Just me and all my friends." She laughed.

Stella didn't smile. She turned her phone toward Lisa. The screen showed a picture of Brianna. She smiled broadly in the shade of an orange-leafed maple. A green scarf was wrapped around her neck and her brown curls were hidden under a matching woolen hat.

"You seen this woman before?"

Lisa sipped her tea again, then put the cup on the floor next to her piano stool. She pulled the phone closer, stared at the screen, then shook her head.

"No. Should I?"

Stella kept her arm extended, pressing the photo toward Lisa. The denial had been quick and confident.

Maybe too quick. "Look again."

Lisa sighed and leaned forward. She scratched her shaven head above her ear. "She's got a strong chin on her. Good for holding a violin. Does she play strings? Is that what this is about?"

If Lisa was hiding something, she was putting it behind a wall made of steel.

Stella brought up the photo of Jane Lin. Jane looked so happy and at ease in this picture, a shot taken somewhere in New York. Stella remembered how she'd seen her last, her head on its side, mouth ajar, eyes trapped forever in a blank, horrific gaze. The body a few feet away, blood puddled next to the severed neck.

"What about her?"

Again, Lisa shook her head. Quick. "No, I've never seen her before either. Are you showing me all your friends? Trying to make me jealous? I've got all the friends I need."

That reply was even faster, even more confident. Lisa looked more comfortable than she did at the start of the conversation.

Stella pushed the phone back into her pocket and rested her arms on the top of the chair again. She glared at Lisa, her patience thinning.

"How are you coping since the death of your father?"

Lisa was bending over, her arms stretching for her tea. She stopped mid-reach. The hesitation was only a split second, but Stella knew the question had punctured Lisa's steely exterior. Then she lifted the drink, and her hand shook just enough that she needed the other one to steady the cup. She shivered, as if they were sitting on the edge of a skating rink.

"I'm fine. Thank you for asking."

Stella said nothing.

She stood and spun the chair around, pushing it back into place among the violinists. Stella's eyes met Stacy's for the briefest of seconds before Ander stood and pushed his chair next to hers.

Stella thanked Lisa for her help.

But the pianist, her face hidden behind her cup, didn't reply.

They left the auditorium as the musicians returned.

As soon as they reentered the foyer, Stella stopped. "She's lying."

Ander nodded, agreeing. "But lying about what?"

"As far as I know, everything. All of it. Certainly, about her father. No one loses their dad and is fine less than two weeks later. No one normal, anyway." She spat out her judgment. "That's just nuts."

"But she wasn't fine, was she? You saw the way her hand shook after you asked her. You rattled her."

"Yeah."

All Stella had wanted to do was provoke Lisa into showing a real, human response. Force her to drop her guard for a moment.

Instead, Lisa had tried to yank her guard up even higher and, in the process, revealed the emotion bubbling beneath the surface.

Stella leaned against the wall, one shoulder blocking the beam of light on the benefit concert's poster. "So why lie about it? Just say you're struggling. Say it's hard, and you miss him. Isn't that what you'd have done? Why is her first reaction to hide the truth?"

Ander crossed his arms over his chest, his typical thinking pose. "Maybe she just didn't want to look vulnerable in front of us?"

"But grief isn't a sign of vulnerability. It's a sign of basic humanity."

"To you. To her, it's a weakness, something she has to conceal. Especially from us."

Stella pushed herself away from the wall and headed to the building's entrance. "I dunno. Call it a hunch, but I think something's off. When the first thing you think of is to hide and lie, something's not right."

Ander followed Stella to the car. "You want to call in 'lying, grieving daughter'?"

Stella opened the passenger's door and sat down sideways, both legs outside the car. No, she didn't want to call it in.

A hunch was too little to go on, but her suspicion was also too strong to ignore. Lisa didn't have an alibi. She had a reason to target FBI family members. She was lying. And the piano tuner was a strange coincidence.

Something else bothered Stella, but she couldn't put her finger on it. Like an earworm she couldn't quite identify.

"Not really. But I'm going to anyway."

She called Slade, putting the phone on speaker.

But before she could start, Slade jumped in, explaining what the forensic team found at Brianna's. "I was just about to call you. Great timing."

Blood that matched Brianna's type was in the living room. And a message, identical to the one chalked over Jane Lin's body, had been scrawled on Brianna's television screen.

Chop, chop, FBI.

When Slade was finished, Stella knew what the earworm was. Lisa's home was a shrine to *Alice in Wonderland*.

"Off with their heads." She whispered the words, almost letting the phone drop.

"What?" Ander and Slade spoke at the same time.

"It's Lisa. I'm sure of it." She turned to Ander. "Remember her house? The chessboard floor? The walls? All the *Alice in Wonderland* dolls? She's wreaking vengeance by becoming the Red Queen. *Off with their heads.*"

Slade's response came as a low whistle followed by a quiet curse. "Jeez, Stella. What am I supposed to do with that?"

"We need a search warrant for her house and car. We need to get into her home and turn it upside down. Brianna could be held up there right now."

"For crying out loud, if you think I'm going to call up a judge and ask for a search warrant because the pianist of the

Kentwood Philharmonic is a Lewis Carroll fan, you're crazier than she is."

"Boss, I'm sure it's her. Check her alibi, see if she's telling the truth about going for a drive this morning. Ping her phone. We can't just let her go."

From the other end of the line came the sound of a long exhalation. "Okay, fine. You might be right. Mac's been trying to dig into that other woman, the one near the school."

"Anne Lawson?"

"Yeah, her. Apparently, Special Agent Chan suspects Anne Lawson did indeed do something nefarious to Mr. Lawson. She's been tracking all of Anne Lawson's drunken escapades."

"Legally?" Stella and Ander exchanged dubious glances.

"Mac didn't press. The long and short of it...Anne Lawson's out. According to Chan, Lawson spends half her time inside a bottle and the other half in a fantasy. She may be a killer, but she's not *this* killer. I've got Chloe and Caleb sweeping the school in case Brianna is there. But that'll take a while. The place is trashed."

"It wouldn't be the school because Lisa knows we found a body there." Stella pressed a hand to her stomach. "How many empty buildings are between here and Brianna's house?"

Ander groaned. "Too many."

It was a rhetorical question, but Stella nodded. "And we have no reason to believe Lisa would have brought Brianna all the way back here. That would be quite the risk, actually, driving over two hours with a hostage. When did the roommates last see Brianna?"

"Yesterday afternoon," Slade said. "They're both out of town for the weekend."

"And we don't know how long Brianna's been missing?"

"No. Last Amanda spoke to her was yesterday afternoon when they made plans to ride horses together."

Stella glanced at Ander and they both turned to stare at the building they'd just exited. There was just one suspect now, and she was on the other side of those concert hall doors.

"What do you want us to do?"

Slade's voice came back clear and firm. "Stay there. Watch the entrance. If she leaves, follow her. If she so much as scratches her ear, I want to know about it. We might not have any evidence yet, but let's make sure she can't do anything to Brianna without us knowing, in case. I'll have Mac check her phone signals. Let's see if she was really out by that bridge, or if she went any farther."

Slade disconnected the call, and Stella sent a message to Stacy.

Don't let her out of your sight.

33

Hagen closed his eyes and dropped his head into his hands. Amanda wrapped her arm around his back. Her fingers rubbed gently between his shoulder blades. It didn't help. Nothing did. The pain, the fear, the anger, they all roiled inside his chest, gripping his lungs and searing the back of his throat.

Brianna was out there somewhere. Maybe dead, murdered in the same brutal way as Jane had been. He rubbed his eyes, trying to erase Jane's mangled body from his memory.

But maybe Brianna was still alive, terrified, and in desperate need of rescue.

And he was here, at Amanda's ranch, waiting for news. Everything was wrong.

Slowly, he opened his eyes again and dropped back onto the sofa.

Even the room, normally so comforting, felt wrong.

The sofa was cream-colored, studded with thick cushions and decorated in a floral pattern appropriate for a quiet country cottage. The fireplace had a black iron grate that

Hagen doubted had ever seen soot. Two oil paintings hung on either side of the mantelpiece, showing horses standing proudly against a southern sky.

This room had always been a place to relax in the evenings with a glass of bourbon.

The space was now a waiting room, a tense spot where every second felt more like a minute.

Clint, Amanda's husband, pushed the den door open with his foot and carried in a tray with a pot of coffee and a pile of cups. His arrival almost made Hagen laugh. Almost.

His brother-in-law's strong chin had three days of stubble. His plaid shirt was tucked into his dark blue jeans. A thin line separated his hair just above his ears, where his hat usually rested.

He should have been out on his horse, rounding up cattle and covering his boots with dust. Instead, he looked like a young cowboy playing the part of a nineteen fifties housewife.

Clint placed the tray on the table just as the crunch of wheels on gravel sounded through the window.

Ignoring the weak, milky coffee Clint poured for him, Hagen shot up and pulled the drapes away from the window.

A police car drew up in front of the stables. A woman emerged from the back seat as soon as the vehicle came to a halt.

Hagen's mother, Nicole, was in her early fifties but seemed older. Her curly brown hair was shot through with gray. The dark slacks she wore were chosen for comfort, not fashion. Her cheeks were red, and her shoulders had the beginnings of a stoop, both the result of too much sustained effort chasing small children around a kindergarten.

But her features were barely lined, and when she was with her friends in a wine bar or attending a barn dance, Hagen had seen the years fall away.

She strode up to the front door of the house, which had been left open—just in case— and a moment later, his mother was in the living room.

"Oh, Ma!" Amanda was out of her seat in an instant. She threw her arms around her mother's shoulders and pulled her into her chest, sobbing.

Hagen put his arms around both of them.

That was his job. It had to be. To reassure everyone everything would be okay. They'd find Brianna and rescue her. Then he'd find the person who'd kidnapped her and tear her into pieces so small, they could blow away in the breeze.

Hagen's mom pulled herself away. "Is there any news?"

Hagen shook his head. "I'm sure they'll tell me as soon as they know anything for sure."

Amanda's forehead creased. She had brown hair that fell in elegant waves between her shoulder blades. She shared Hagen's square chin, and when she frowned, a small dent appeared above the bridge of her nose. That indent appeared now, an invitation to dive into her darkest thoughts.

"And if they're not sure? If they're not telling us anything, what does that mean? Does that mean they don't know where she is? Hagen, what's going on?"

Hagen kept his hand on his mother's back, as much to reassure himself as to reassure her.

"When they know something for certain, they'll tell us. We have to trust them. We have to. The team looking for Brianna, they're the best. I know them. They'll find her."

Hagen's mom patted his shoulder gently. "I'm sure they will, hun. I'm sure they will."

Hagen tried to smile. The effort didn't entirely work, but he hoped at least he was able to summon an expression of confidence. "They *will*. You know how many people we've found like this? It's what the FBI is trained to do. We *know* what we're doing."

The words came out of his mouth as easily as drawing his badge from his pocket. Reassuring others came easily.

And yet, how many times have we let people down? How many times have we turned up too late?

Benji Kopp and Tyson Ragen. Tiffany Wright and Darlene Medina-Martinson. The Bisgards. The list was too long.

In every case they'd tackled, they'd lost people before they'd cracked it. They'd pulled bodies out of dumpsters, picked up corpses by the roadside, processed murder scenes in family homes.

Jane Lin was only the latest. And there was no reason to assume she'd be the last.

Brianna could be next.

Hagen's stomach clenched. His throat tightened. He turned away from his mother and sister and walked to the front window. He wanted to be sick.

He couldn't lose Brianna. Not her.

This is all my fault. I should have taken better care of her. I should have brought her here as soon as we found Jane and stayed here to protect them both.

Hagen strode toward the door. His back was straight, his eyes unblinking. He knew what he was going to do. The one thing he could do. That he had to do.

He needed a job done. He needed it done properly. So he needed to do it himself.

Without stopping to say goodbye to anyone, Hagen headed outside, straight to the cruiser. "Don't let them out of your sight."

The officer propped a hand on his weapon. "I won't."

With a nod, Hagen climbed into his Corvette.

Gravel sprayed against the wall of the house as the engine roared.

34

Outside the philharmonic, Stella sipped her cocoa and sized up the last donut. Ander pushed the box closer. "Go on. You know you want to."

She did want to, but she also knew she shouldn't. The one donut she'd already eaten was plenty and probably too much.

"Nah, I'm good."

A sharp shriek of violins tuning up shot out of Ander's phone. "I wish we could watch the performance live rather than listen secondhand through Stacy's phone."

Inside the building, Stacy was onstage with Lisa Kerne. For the past few hours, the woman had been within her sight line, with Ander and Stella backing Stacy up. If Lisa made one wrong move, they'd be all over her.

Ander shrugged and stuffed the fried dough into his mouth. It was his third since they'd left the concert hall and taken up their position in Ander's car.

He mumbled something through a full mouth, prompting Stella to lower her cup and lick the froth from her upper lip.

"What did you say?"

Ander chewed and swallowed. He nodded in the direction of the concert hall on the other side of the road. "I was just wondering how much they paid for their tickets."

An oversized SUV pulled into the parking lot, offloading a couple of passengers who joined the throng, making their way up the broad steps to the doors.

The men wore light suits and ties, their jackets far too hot for early evening in a Tennessee summer. The women's long dresses were sleeveless or backless and often both. Whether that lack of material was intended to keep them cool or to better show off their pearls and gold, Stella really wasn't sure. Everyone attending the concert seemed to be decked out in jewels and designer wear that would set Stella back three months' worth of her government salary.

Stella shrugged, taking a quick sip of her cocoa. "I've no idea. Whatever they paid, it's far more than you or I could afford."

"But it's all for such a good cause."

"Ha." Stella sipped her cocoa again. The drink, which Ander had picked up from a convenience store, was better than she'd expected. The sweetness took the edge off the dullness of the stakeout. "Because keeping musicians ready to entertain the rich folk of Kentwood is an important cause."

"It is if you live in Kentwood."

Ander tossed the empty donut box onto the back seat, where it joined empty paper bags and snack wrappers.

A black Corvette pulled into the parking lot and disgorged a man in his early sixties with thin gray hair. He had to wait while his wife disentangled herself from the car's low seat and rearranged her chiffon dress.

The Corvette made Stella think of Hagen.

He was at his sister's ranch, as he should be. The best place he could be right now was with his family. Knowing he was there gave Stella a sense of relief. As long as Hagen was guarding his family, the killer wouldn't be able to target Amanda or his mother.

And Hagen wouldn't be out killing anyone for revenge.

Anyone setting foot on that ranch with the intention of doing harm would more than meet their match. Hagen would blow them away as soon as he saw them. And this time, they'd deserve it.

He had to be hurting. To think his sister was being held somewhere was bad enough. The fear she might already be dead must be tearing him apart.

No. She's alive. We'll find her.

But to just sit and wait for news must be unbearable. Stella knew Hagen well enough to understand he'd be straining at the leash, bursting to leave the ranch and do something, anything, to find the person responsible for his sister's disappearance.

His forbearance would be the biggest battle he'd ever had to face.

Stella wasn't sure he could win. She sighed deeply.

"You okay?" Ander looked worried.

"Hm? Yeah. Just thinking about Hagen."

Ander and Hagen were close friends, used to spending their evenings shooting the breeze over beers and ball games.

"The best thing we can do for Hagen is to catch the bastard who took his sister and do it fast. The sooner Lisa makes a move, the sooner we'll have her."

"We just need evidence."

"Lisa'll give us the evidence. The moment she goes to deal with Brianna, we'll make our move. We'll have her then. Red-handed."

"And if she's already dealt with Brianna?" Just saying the words twisted Stella's stomach. She was sure Ander was worried that they were too late. But neither of them had spoken those thoughts aloud. Until now.

Ander stirred his cup, staring deep into the swirling liquid. "I don't want to think about that. If she's murdered Brianna, I'll kill her myself."

The anger at the back of Ander's voice didn't sound like Hagen's. There was none of the venom or determination that drove Hagen's words when he talked about his dad's killer.

Ander was angry now, but when the time came, he was no more likely to kill Lisa Kerne than Stella was.

He swept some spilled donut sugar from the top of his pants. "Anyway, we have to assume Brianna's alive. She wasn't killed at her house and Lisa wouldn't have had time to kill her and dispose of the body before she arrived for the auditions. All was clear at Merys High School. Stacy has eyes on her, and she can't leave the building without us seeing her."

"Which means Brianna's holed up somewhere. If only we had some idea where. Do we have a warrant yet to check Lisa's trunk?"

"Not yet." Ander's eyes lit up at the idea of doing something besides sitting across from the philharmonic building. "Do you remember what she drives?"

Stella grinned, knowing they were thinking the same thing. Warrant or no warrant, they could put eyes on the vehicle. "I think so. I can also have Mac run car registrations in her name. Then we can go to the employee parking lot."

"Deal."

Stella lifted her phone.

"You going to call Slade first? Tell him what we're thinking?"

"Actually, I was going to call Hagen first. If waiting like this is killing us, what the hell's it doing to him?"

She dialed. The phone rang and rang. Stella frowned. Surely, Hagen wouldn't be more than two rings away from his phone at a time like this.

"He's not answering."

Ander pulled out his own phone. "That's strange. You'd think the dude would be just waiting for a call. I'll try Amanda."

Amanda's phone barely completed its first ring before she answered.

"Ander? What's happening?"

Ander and Stella exchanged a confused look. "Nothing, sorry. Nothing new yet. I was just trying to reach Hagen. He's not answering his phone."

"He's not with you? I figured he was on his way to you. I thought that was why you were calling. He called an officer to guard me and Mom, then shot out of here like a bat out of hell."

Stella sank into the car seat. Hagen had broken.

35

The new girl made me smudge my eyeliner. I was giving myself a cat eye when she sidled up next to my table in the shared dressing room.

Her arm extended as straight as a crane as she introduced herself. "Hello, I'm Joy. The new cellist. You must be Lisa Kerne. I am *such* a fan."

I gave her the smallest of smiles and shook her palm briefly with the tips of my thumb and fingers. When I turned back to the mirror, I saw the line I'd drawn along my eyelashes had risen too high.

"Dammit."

I yanked out a wipe and cleaned the mess she'd caused.

Joy didn't notice my irritation. She rested a shoulder against the side of the vending machine, as though I'd invited her to hang around and shoot the breeze. I'd done no such thing. Like I wanted to chat with a third cello.

Or with any of them.

As though their complaints and weekend gossip meant anything to me. I had other things on my mind, including the girl in the basement practice room twenty feet below where I was currently sitting.

Not to mention the bag stashed under my makeup table, holding a bloodstained axe.

Joy didn't take the hint at all.

"And thank you *so* much for playing at my audition this afternoon. I heard they had to call you in on short notice. *So* inconsiderate. You were probably enjoying your day off too. A well-earned day off, I'm sure." She tilted her head, making herself comfortable in a conversation I had no interest in. "Were you doing anything nice?"

I hesitated, holding the wipe half an inch from the side of my eye. "Uh-huh. I was having the time of my life. Now if you don't mind, I'm—"

"Well, thank you for giving up what you were doing to help me out. I mean...I know you didn't come in to help *me*... but you did help me." Joy lowered her voice. "Frankly, if it hadn't been for your beautiful playing, I doubt I'd have gotten this job at all. I was so nervous."

Someone behind Joy laughed. One of the trombone players.

They were watching, waiting for me to tell Joy, in a voice louder than any of their stupid marching band instruments, to get the hell away from me. I didn't want to give them the satisfaction.

Ignoring my new friend, I reached for the eyeliner again and carefully drew a little upward flick. Joy watched me closely.

"Oh, that's beautiful. You're very good at that. You could have been a makeup artist, you know. And your hair! My gosh. So brave."

Another snigger from a French horn.

I ran my fingers across the shaved side of my head. To tell

the truth, the third cello's compliments on my hair did warm me.

I'd chosen the style on a whim.

Sitting in the salon, the hairdresser had rested her fingers on my head and prattled on about where she was going on vacation. She wanted California. Her boyfriend fancied Mexico, but she was afraid of food poisoning. Like I cared. Irritated with her constant gabbing, I grabbed the electric razor, slid it down the side of my head, and left her ten bucks on the table. I'd kept the style ever since.

Joy was the first person to ever compliment me on it, though.

I lowered my hand and checked my eyeliner. The curve was looking fine now.

"I can do the same to you if you want." I kept my eyes on the mirror as I spoke. "Shave both sides of your head. Hey, maybe I should shave your nut entirely. Get rid of all that messy long hair. What do you think?"

She swallowed so hard she almost choked. Her hand drifted to her mousy brown-blond nest. "I…I…I don't think that would suit me."

"Aw, come on now. It'll be fun."

"I really don't…I'm really not brave enough for anything like that." She bent toward me and lowered her voice. "I mean your courage is incredible. To come back here and play this concert, dedicated to the man your father is accused of killing. I am so in awe of you, Lisa."

I didn't move.

A chill passed down my spine and settled into my stomach like the ice in a double bourbon. Did she mean what she'd just said? She looked sincere. No one knew better than me that human sympathy was as rare in this world as a three-legged chicken. Yet the cellist's eyes had a real softness to them when she spoke. Like she really empathized with my predicament, like she understood my situation entirely, like she could burrow into my very bones and feel the pain and the rage burning inside me.

And the fear.

There was plenty of fear running through me too.

That Yates girl in the basement wouldn't stay unnoticed forever. If I didn't deal with her soon, if I didn't put her away, someone would find her. Then they'd find me.

The door opened. The stage manager poked his head into the room, his headset making him look like some kind of alien invader.

"Places, please, everyone."

The others called, "Thank you, places."

Joy gave me one last smile and went to fetch her instrument. I closed my eyes and took a deep breath, willing my nerves to settle. I'd been almost relaxed until she'd spoken about my father.

Now that unsteadiness returned. My fingers trembled. I could have been a ten-year-old child forced to play her first proper solo in front of her class.

Although, when I was a kid, I'd never been nervous before a performance. On the contrary, I'd always been ready to disappear into the music, to lose myself behind the piano.

The rest of the orchestra took their things and headed for the stage.

I waited in the room, alone. Just me and my new toy rabbit, sitting there at the end of the table, staring at me. Blame in his eyes.

"Oh dear, oh dear." That was what he seemed to say. "You ought to be ashamed of yourself, a great girl like you. Stop this moment, I tell you."

I curled my hands into tight fists. I wouldn't let my fingers shake no matter how much they wanted to. *I* controlled *them*.

Nothing controlled me.

With my knuckles as white as his unblemished fur, I left the room and moved into the wings, waiting for my cue.

On the stage, the spotlight beamed on the conductor. He addressed the audience.

"And it's my great pleasure to announce tonight's pianist." He paused, then dramatically bellowed my name to the great and the good of Kentwood. "Lisa Kerne!"

The applause was scattered. Instead of the wall of crashing sound I was accustomed to receiving, I got nothing more than a few polite handclaps from one side of the hall and a few more from the other. They faded quickly and were replaced by the harsher sounds of coughs and throat clearing.

For the first time, I heard my own footsteps creaking on the wooden boards. All the way across the stage, my hands remained balled up, my short fingernails pressed into my palms.

A benefit in the name of a man who'd humiliated my father and driven him mad enough to commit murder.

They'd insisted I play in it.

This was some kind of cruel and unusual punishment.

No wonder the audience wanted no part of it.

And neither did I.

In silence, I dragged out the stool and sat facing the keyboard.

For the first time in more years than I could recall, my heart thumped in my chest as I stared at the instrument. I didn't want to touch it.

I just wanted to run off that stage, race down to that basement rehearsal room, and hack that girl's head off with a solid whack of my axe.

Nothing would give me greater satisfaction.

Keeping the image of the Yates girl bloodied and dead in

my mind, I straightened my back and flexed my fingers. With my hands stretched and my fingers splayed, I was still in control.

But as soon as I relaxed and held my wrists over the keyboard, anticipating the fall of the conductor's baton, my digits found their own desire again. Instead of waiting patiently for the plunge, they seemed to dance above the instrument.

My head danced with them. Usually at this time, my mind would be on the first note, knowing that the moment the sound came, the floor would open, and I would fall into the music. The chords and rhythms would build walls around me until there was nothing but cadences, rising and falling.

But as I sat there, aware that the third cello's eyes were on me like some kind of hungry puppy, my thoughts drifted. They left the auditorium and floated back down the stairs to that basement room.

As soon as the concert ended—that was when I'd deal with her. I'd get my revenge, and what I'd do to her would be sweeter than even the most heart-stopping symphony.

The conductor beat me in.

My fingers pressed the keys. The magic didn't happen. The floor didn't open and drop me into harmony. I had to think about what I was doing.

I forced my fingers to slow down and brought them back to the right tempo. Holding the image of a soon-to-be-dead Brianna Yates soothed me some.

The remaining pieces went smoothly enough, but I'd never been so glad to reach an intermission.

In the dressing room, I found Joy waiting next to my table. I lowered my head and pushed down my irritation. I didn't want to speak to anyone, not now. Not after that performance.

She smiled when she saw me and reached into her bag to

pull out a small toy cat. She rested the fluffy animal on top of her instrument case and pointed at my toy rabbit.

"We kinda match. Except mine's a cat, of course. Like the Cheshire Cat in *Alice in Wonderland*."

The last time I'd played so poorly, a college recital just after my father went missing, I didn't leave my room for four days. I buried myself in my favorite book and tried to call my father every hour.

Hearing Joy mention *Alice in Wonderland* was like a hot drink on a frozen day, warming inside and instantly calming.

I sat at my table and checked my makeup. "You read that book?"

"Read it? I love it." Joy leaned closer. "I think the conductor does too. The way he kept time in that first half, I think he's been stealing a go on the caterpillar's hookah."

The warmth spread. The burden weighing on my shoulders since my father's death shrank a little. I wasn't sure whether Joy really blamed the conductor for my mistakes or was just tactful enough to know what to say.

But the effect was the same. Her words made me feel better.

Joy stroked the top of her cat. "Hey, do members of the orchestra go out for a drink after the concert? Frankly, I could do with a shot of something right now, but I can wait until the show's over."

I turned back to the mirror above my dressing table. "I've no idea. And I really don't care. As soon as this concert ends, I'm out of here."

Joy gave me an uneasy smile, but I ignored it.

I had something better to do when this concert ended.

And what I'd planned would hit the spot harder than any drink a bar could offer.

The stage manager opened the door again. "Five minutes, everyone."

36

Stella sat in Ander's car, phone to her ear. She listened, one knee rocking with impatience. The ringing continued, the beeps stretching on until, without warning, they stopped entirely. Again.

She swore quietly.

Ander approached her open window from the parking lot. Mac hadn't gotten back to them with Lisa Kerne's car registration, so he'd gone into the employee lot and banged on all the trunks while she continued to call Hagen. They were pretty sure she drove a Honda, but they weren't taking any chances that she'd traded vehicles.

"Still nothing?"

Stella shook her head. "Hagen can't have turned his phone off. He's just ignoring me. You?"

"If Brianna is in any of those trunks, she's not in any condition to answer."

"Well, that's not great news." Stella lowered her phone and tapped it twice against her leg, as though she could shake a response out of the device. "He's not answering your calls either?"

"I don't think he'll be answering any of us right now."

Ander rested his elbow on the bottom of the open window and looked out over the road. Behind them, a small park with rolling hills lit only by the moon made the perfect spot for daytime picnicking.

In front of them, ground-mounted spotlights cast pale blue cones over the white walls of the music center. The doors were closed now. But the sound of the orchestra was just barely audible, a distant drumming interjected by the trumpets and strings.

Somewhere in there, Lisa Kerne played the piano, a performance Stella and Ander had heard only recently and enjoyed greatly.

Now, when thinking about Lisa Kerne, Stella felt sick and afraid for Brianna. There was no beauty left in Lisa or her music at all.

The music stopped. The crash of applause seeped through the building's walls like waves around rocks.

Ander's eyes were fixed firmly on the entrance. "We could call Slade. Have him call Hagen. I don't know if even Hagen would be dumb enough to filter out the SSA."

Stella lifted her cocoa from the holder. The cup was empty. All that remained were the oversweet dregs where sugar had collected in the chocolate at the bottom. She tipped the cup back anyway, hoping the familiar taste would give her some of the reassurance she needed.

It didn't.

She dropped the cup back into the holder.

"What if he does?"

"What if he does what?"

"Ghost Slade."

Ander shook his head, unwilling to entertain the idea. "Now *that* would be dumb. Dude just finished being under investigation for killing Boris Kerne. That all came out fine in the wash, but ignoring his SSA? That's not a good move."

"No. It isn't." Stella tugged at her ear stud. "Might be enough to end him at the Bureau. Or at least put him behind a desk for the rest of his career. Which, let's face it, for Hagen, it would be the same thing."

Ander said nothing, which was all the agreement Stella needed.

She pulled harder at her ear stud, turning over ideas in her mind. Hagen was almost certainly on his way here, and he wasn't going to politely take over the stakeout.

He was going to burst into that auditorium and confront Lisa Kerne. He might even do it onstage, storming up in front of the audience.

Stella didn't want to imagine how that confrontation would go.

When they faced what looked like a lethal threat, he didn't flinch from reaching for his weapon.

Hagen, armed, angry, and desperate, would be a dangerous man.

Stella lifted her phone again.

Ander frowned. "You calling Slade?"

"No."

She waited for the phone to connect. The line rang twice before she heard Dan Garcia's familiar voice.

"Stella. What's up?"

"I need a favor, Dan. A big one."

There was silence for a moment as Dan weighed this information before sighing. "What do you need?"

"I'm going to send you the make, model, and reg of a car. I need you to pull it over."

Dan made the low growl he always made when his suspicions rose. "What's the driver done?"

"You can do him for speeding. I guarantee he's not

sticking to the limit. Also, I'm pretty sure his choice of radio station is criminal."

"Uh-huh." Dan fell silent for a moment. "You're scared of what he's *gonna* do, aren't you?"

"I think so."

"This that new partner of yours?"

"Hagen, yeah. We think Lisa Kerne, the pianist at the Kentwood Philharmonic, might be responsible for that body you found at the school. And it's also possible she's holding Hagen's sister somewhere."

From the other end of the line came the sound of a slow, deep intake of breath.

Stella imagined Dan sitting in his car, stroking his mustache, and working his way through his options until he settled on a course of action. He was always so calm and level-headed. She trusted him. And he trusted her. She'd seen that on their toughest case when they'd tried to talk down a couple of gun-wielding criminals.

"In that case, I can't blame him for being a dumb hothead. Not sure I'd behave any different, if I'm honest. Where's your boy heading?"

"Toward us. We're staking out the philharmonic, otherwise we'd stop him ourselves. We think he's heading this way from the direction of Stonevale."

Through the phone speaker, Dan's police siren fired up. The wail reassured Stella. Someone with responsibility was taking the problem seriously. "I'm on my lonesome today, which is probably a stroke of luck, considering the amount of trouble you're getting me into. Send me the details. Let's see if I can cool him down before his hot head does something he regrets in the cold light of day. Well, night."

Stella smiled. "Thanks. I really appreciate it."

She closed the line and typed a text to her former partner the details of Hagen's Corvette. Ander watched her.

"At least Hagen's car is hard to miss."

"Yeah, but it's also hard to stop."

Stella hit send.

"If we were worrying about Hagen ghosting Slade, I'm not sure what odds we should give him on pulling over for a siren and a flashing light." Ander shook his head, irritated and worried about his friend and colleague. "Shoot. Hagen's gonna get himself into a whole world of trouble."

Stella reached for her cocoa before remembering, again, that she'd finished it. As she dropped the cup back into the holder, a police siren screamed on her right.

Dan Garcia's unmarked car shot past her. The sight made Stella smile. The number of times she'd sat next to Dan when he'd turned on the lights and floored the gas were countless.

"Man, if anyone can catch up with him, Dan—"

"Hagen's right there."

Ander pointed up the road to the left. In the distance, just in front of the horizon line, a cherry-red Corvette raced toward the music center.

The car must have been doing close to a hundred in a thirty-five-mile-per-hour business zone. The engine's rumble grew louder with every second.

Without thinking, Stella reached for her phone again and called Hagen.

Again, the line rang, and again, no one answered.

Dan must've seen him because the unmarked cop car screeched to a halt, its back end sliding across the road, blocking the lanes in each direction. This wasn't Dan's first roadblock.

Hagen's Corvette bore down toward Stella's former partner. Hagen was visible now in the driver's seat. She imagined both hands white-knuckled at the top of the steering wheel, his face utterly focused.

The door of the police car opened. Dan Garcia stepped

out, unhurried, unconcerned.

The Corvette sped toward him.

Dan closed the car door, stood before it, and crossed his arms. Only about two hundred yards of road and the power of nearly five hundred horses separated him and Hagen.

Hagen bore down. Dan didn't move. Stella leapt out of the car and waved her arms.

"Stop! For chrissakes, Hagen. Stop!"

She was vaguely aware of Ander on the other side of the car doing the same, but it took her a second longer to realize she'd forgotten to breathe.

If Hagen doesn't stop, he'll kill Dan. I'll have killed Dan.
I'll have killed Hagen.
I'll—

The Corvette tires screamed. Smoke poured from wheel wells. A thick black cloud rose from the back of the car. The Corvette kept coming, still moving in a straight line, its back wheels sliding first one way, then the other. The car fishtailed directly toward Dan Garcia.

Her former partner stood still as a stone sculpture.

The front fender came to a jolting halt about three inches from Dan Garcia's knees.

Stella breathed out and heard Ander do the same. Slowly, her hands shaking, she lowered her arms as Hagen emerged from his vehicle.

Dan Garcia still didn't move. He kept his eyes on Hagen when he spoke. "Sir, do you have any idea how fast you were going?"

Stella found the energy to run.

Ander sprinted behind her.

The air was filled with the stink of burning rubber. Hagen's face was pale, as though he only now understood what would have happened if he hadn't hit the brakes in the nick of time.

Color returned to his cheeks at the sight of Stella.

He looked from her to the music center. She saw him make the wrong decision.

Hagen broke into a sprint toward the philharmonic entrance.

"Police!" Dan shouted. "Stop."

Stella knew shouting wouldn't stop him. With a decent head start, she put her head down and raced to cut him off. She got ahead of him, and stood, arms wide, ribs screaming. "Hagen! Stop!"

He drew up at her voice. His eyes darted between Stella and the front of the building again.

Hagen didn't speak.

Stella snapped her fingers. "Hagen!"

A softness came into his eyes, as though he was seeing her for the first time.

Stella seized the opportunity. "Hagen, listen to me. Stacy's in there. We've got eyes on Kerne. She can't do anything without us knowing. You've got to trust Stacy, Hagen. Trust her and trust me. We've got this. Together."

Hagen's jaw set. In the blue light illuminating the front of the music center, his brow darkened above his eyes.

"She's got Brianna."

"If she *does* have Brianna, we need her to lead us to *where*. You know that, Hagen. You've got to be patient. I know it's hard, but I also know you can do it. If anyone knows about being patient, it's you."

She looked into his eyes. In this light, the green of his irises was entirely absent. All Stella saw were two dark holes in a face creased with rage and determination.

But slowly, that fury softened, smoothing out his features. Hagen drew back. He took a deep breath.

"Patient? I think I've been patient long enough."

37

I dragged the cotton round beneath my eye, checked the dark mascara smudge the pad removed, then tried again. There was nothing left on my face now except embarrassment, but I didn't want to leave the dressing room. I planned to be the last one here, the only one in the building.

The others weren't making it easy for me, though. Almost all the performers had left, but Joy, the third cello, was still in the room, chatting with two of the violins. I couldn't hear everything they said, but I could tell they weren't talking about me and that was good enough.

Sometimes, Joy glanced at me as they laughed. She looked like she was inviting me to come and join them, but I had no intention of doing any such thing. Never chatted with anyone in the orchestra before and saw no reason to start now.

I just wanted them all to leave. I wanted them to get the heck out of there and leave me alone. In the building. There were things I had to do.

Another peal of laughter spilled from what remained of the strings, and I threw the cotton round into the garbage.

Enough.

They weren't going anywhere. I could see that. They were the kind of people who would stay in a restaurant while the servers piled the chairs, and the cleaners swabbed the floor around their feet. I couldn't wait that long. I shoved my toy rabbit into my bag, hoping the fluff would cover any sign of the axe underneath it, and stood up.

"Good night." I gave them just the smallest of waves as I passed.

"You're leaving now?" That was Joy, of course. She was the only one in the group who'd spoken to me all evening. "Why don't you wait a little longer? We'll all leave together. Maybe we can find a bar or something, get to know each other a little."

The faces of the two violinists blanched at that invitation. I saw what they thought, no matter how hard they tried to hide it.

"No. Thank you."

I didn't slow down, not even when Joy reached for her instrument case. Before she'd managed to throw her own toy cat into her bag, I was in the passageway and pulling the door closed behind me.

The way to the front of the building was to my right. That would take me out onto the road. The exit to the back parking lot was to the left.

Halfway down that corridor were the stairs to the basement practice room.

I hung a left and moved fast. One of the advantages of being a pianist is that you don't have to lug around a big, heavy instrument like a cellist. Just a bag with a toy rabbit. And a good, sharp axe.

By the time the changing room door opened again, I was already halfway down the stairs to the basement. The backstage door, which everyone always ignored, was closed behind me, shrouding me in darkness.

The air was cold. The staircase dropped straight from the passageway for about ten feet, then turned left for another ten feet or so. The chill from the air-conditioning always collected down here. It was like stepping inside a walk-in freezer, going into the percussion room. I crouched in the darkness, listening for footsteps, and a shiver ran down my back.

Despite the chill, I wasn't going anywhere. I would stay hidden until everyone was out of the building. Once they were gone, I'd have this place all to myself and I'd be free to make any sweet music I wanted in the practice room.

The audience reaction would be glorious.

Hagen Yates sobbing and bawling, broken and defeated. That noise would be more welcome than any ovation I'd ever received.

And the rhythm I would make. One chop, or maybe two or three, like last time, depending on how tough that young neck was. I'd get such sweet revenge from every swing of the axe.

I could hear it already. The *swoosh* the blade made as it broke through the air. The *squirt* of the first bloody stream jetting out of her neck and striking the walls. The soft *squelch* of tissue tearing, and the *clang* of the blade finally striking the floor.

And another as I swung again.

Thump. Thump.

The sound came from behind me. I didn't move, uncertain whether I'd really heard it. Surely, I wasn't imagining things. I wasn't crazy. I was almost sure I wasn't.

Thump. Thump. Thump.

There it was again. Definitely not my imagination. The noise was soft. Less like the metal head of an axe striking a concrete floor and more like the heel of a bare foot pounding against a drum. It came again.

Thump. Thump.

I smiled. Like a foot on a drum? Through that thick metal door, the noise was more like a rabbit's foot beating on a plush rug. There was no way anyone upstairs could hear that pathetic sound.

She'd probably been making that noise for hours.

A few more minutes and everyone upstairs would be gone. That was when I'd have this whole place to myself. And I'd do all the sweet, beautiful things I wanted to do.

As I forged my path of revenge.

38

Stella placed her hands on Hagen's shoulders and stared straight into his eyes. "You need to be patient a little longer. You *can't* go in there. You'll blow everything. If you grab Lisa Kerne and she clams up, we'll never find Brianna. We've got to trust Stacy. She'll follow Kerne, and Kerne will lead us to Brianna. That's the only way to do this."

Hagen closed his eyes. When he opened them, he didn't seem to see Stella at all. His face was aimed at the music center, but his mind appeared to be somewhere else.

Ander approached cautiously, standing next to Hagen and Stella. "Let me drive you back to the ranch, man. Your sister and your mother need you. That's where your place is right now. We can cover everything here, but only *you* can look after your family."

Reminding Hagen of his family was a bold step. Remembering that he wasn't protecting his other sister and mother would either send him back to the ranch or make him even more determined to let nothing stand in the way of finding Brianna. Stella wasn't sure which way he would go.

Hagen's forehead creased. He took a deep breath and

lowered his head. The tension in Stella's chest eased slightly. They were getting through. Ander's mention of Hagen's family had pulled him away.

Dan Garcia rolled his car to a stop, got out nice and easy, stood opposite Ander, and ran a thumb down the end of his salt-and-pepper mustache. "You should listen to them, Agent. That's some good advice right there. Go be with your folks. That's your job now."

"Y'hear that?" Ander hooked a thumb toward the police officer. "He's not even going to give you a ticket. That's an offer you really don't want to refuse, Hagen. Not at the speed you were going."

Dan's eyebrows rose. "Now, I didn't say that."

Detective Garcia climbed back into his car and, with his window already down, rested an elbow on the door.

"But I'll give you a pass this time. Christmas in July. Who'd a thunk it? Don't make me change my mind, now."

The edge of Hagen's lip rose slightly, but if he was about to smile, the shift in mood didn't last. As soon as his gaze landed on the music center again, his eyes narrowed, and his chest rose and fell rhythmically.

Hagen's silence was horribly unnerving. Stella gripped his shoulders tighter. "Hagen! Cut this shit out. Stacy's got eyes on Kerne. I'll get Chloe up here to replace Ander. If there's anything to report, anything at all, Stacy will call Slade, and he'll send us in. Until then, you need to get the hell out of here and go back to the ranch. Your sister's probably going crazy wondering where you are."

Hagen took a deep breath and nodded. "Yeah, okay."

Stella sighed with relief, fear falling from her like the end of a dark dream. They were there. At last, she'd gotten through.

Hagen would soon be on his way back, and she could

focus again on dealing with Lisa Kerne. She wouldn't have to worry anymore about what Hagen might or might not do.

She patted his right shoulder twice and released her grip.

Together, the three of them made their way back to the 'Vette, directing Hagen to the passenger seat of his own vehicle.

Ander rubbed his hands together. "Ooh, I get to drive the Corvette today." He climbed into the driver's seat and called through the window toward the police car, who'd "escorted" them, driving at snail's pace, back to Hagen's car.

"Hey, Dan, we still get a pass on speeding?"

Dan shook his head. "Nope. You drive real slow and easy now, like a good boy. Anyone in uniform has to pull over that thing again, and I'll make sure whoever's driving gets themselves—"

He stopped talking as Ander's phone rang. He put the speaker to his ear, but even from five feet away, Stella heard Slade's low voice.

"Just got word from Stacy. She's lost sight of Lisa Kerne. She thinks she's still in the concert hall and that she's holding Brianna there. But Stacy doesn't know where. She's looking for her. You need to move in."

Stella looked up. Hagen was already out of the car and racing toward the building.

39

Brianna's hands were tied behind her back. The tape over her mouth stank of glue, sweat, and plastic. Her legs were taped together at the ankles, but if she bent her knees and kicked, she could slam the back of her bare heels into whatever stood beyond her feet.

She kicked again.

Thump. Thump. Thump.

The noise echoed through the darkness. Only silence followed.

Her left cheek was sore and sticky where it rested against the concrete floor. Damp dust scoured her skin. Her right temple pulsed with a sharp, aching pain.

She couldn't tell how long she'd lain there. A woman arrived at her house and asked for help, she remembered that. The memory of the blow to her head was sharp and solid and made her wince every time the recollection returned.

But she did not know how long she'd been out, how much time had passed since she'd regained consciousness, or where she was. The room was pitch black.

Killer Encore

There'd been music earlier. Faint and muffled, but she was sure she'd heard something that sounded liked an orchestra. Or perhaps she'd been dreaming. Now she heard nothing except her own breath against the stone floor and her feet slapping into something hard and hollow behind her.

She tried again.

Thump. Thump.

Silence.

A tear came, creeping from her right eye, rolling over the bridge of her nose. And with that tear came anger. Rage at the madwoman who'd attacked her and fury, too, at her brother, who was supposed to be rescuing her. He was in the FBI. He was a law enforcement officer who protected and saved members of the public every day.

And he wasn't helping his own sister!

Come on, Hagen. Where the hell are you? Get your ass here already!

Brianna struggled against the tape that bound her. She twisted her wrists until the skin on her arms burned and her shoulders were almost numb with pain. Nothing helped. The tape was strong. The pain in her arms, her wrists, her head, stronger still.

She relaxed and let her shoulder and her cheek sink onto the floor. The concrete was cool, and while the dirt chafed against her skin, it didn't sear like the tape, which wanted to slice into her very bones.

Eee-eeak.

A door opened, creating a screech akin to a young girl screaming. About three yards in front of her, a rectangle of dim, gray light stretched across the floor. For the first time, Brianna could see where she was.

The room was smaller than she'd imagined. The far corner held parts of a drum kit. Two snare drums tilted on their stands. A cymbal looked like it had taken too many blows to the rim and stood at a sharp angle like a badly thrown frisbee. One stand had a leg that was bent and broken while a bass drum sat sideways against the wall behind her feet. So that was what she'd been banging with her trussed-up feet. No wonder her attempts to call for help had sounded so…musical.

She must have been in some kind of rehearsal room, a place where trainee drummers were sent to make a racket away from sensitive ears, which also explained why no one had heard her kicking, even against the bottom of the drum. And why she'd heard music earlier.

At least I'm not mad, then. At least not that.

Eee-eeak.

The noise came again, and the rectangle of gray light grew and widened. At the door's entrance stood a silhouette. The figure wasn't tall or muscular, and the person in the doorway didn't move or speak. They just stood there, surveying the room.

"Hnn. Hnnn."

Brianna tried to shout. She rocked on the floor.

Untie me! Let me out of here, you loon!

The woman from earlier swung the door open and strode into the room, flipping on a light switch as she did.

Brianna sensed her crouching in front of prostrate form before her eyes focused in the dim, dusty, artificial light.

When she spoke, her voice was slow and even. "Awake now, are you?"

For a moment, Brianna wondered whether perhaps she wasn't. Maybe her phone would ring soon, waking her up and forcing her to explain to Amanda why she'd slept through the entire morning and missed their lunch at the ranch. But the pain in her head and her right arm were real, and the dust on her cheek itched and tickled her nose. She was conscious and awake, and she was sure her blood pressure was elevated, and her heart rate was through the roof.

The woman turned on the flashlight on her phone. The angle of the light brought her face into sharp relief.

It was her, the woman who'd turned up on her doorstep, who'd pleaded for help, then smacked the back of Brianna's head with an instrument as hard and heavy as a hammer when Brianna had risen to fetch the first aid kit. A burst of fear sent nausea rising from her stomach. She had to close her eyes for a moment to force the bile and acid back down.

The woman spoke again. "Good. I'm glad you're awake. I'd hate for you to sleep through everything I'm about to do to you."

Do to me?

Brianna shook. She couldn't stop. What began as a tremble grew to spasms that scraped her cheek against the floor and set her teeth chattering.

The woman ignored her reaction. "Oh, yeah. Would have been a real shame for you to have missed out. Now, look at this."

She lowered the bag on her shoulder to the floor. Unzipping the top, she took out a toy rabbit.

Brianna would have laughed if the tape hadn't held her mouth in place. The rabbit was cute, with soft fur, overly long ears, and a small pink nose. If this was all she'd been trussed up to see, the woman in front of her was as mad as a hatter and as harmless as that bunny. But she knew differently and had a pounding head to prove it.

The woman grinned and put the rabbit back in the bag. "Not this. *This*." She reached into the bag again and pulled out an axe.

Brianna's dry throat became even drier. Her heart rate doubled. Her respiration increased.

The wooden handle was almost two feet long. The curved

blade stretched about four inches wide. Dark spots decorated the top of the wood, as though it had recently been used and not cleaned. The woman held the axe from the very bottom of the haft so that it seemed to sit uncomfortably in her hand. She stood straight, letting the blade hang next to her knees.

Nothing Brianna had ever experienced had prepared her for a moment like this. She imagined, in fleeting images, the swing of the axe slicing through her limbs. The ulna and radius in her forearms would put up little resistance. A single swipe would cut clean through them. The femur bone in her thigh would probably need a couple of strong chops. Her ankle bones would take no effort at all.

She could imagine those things, but she couldn't believe them. No one would do such a thing. No one had a reason to do such a thing to her.

And yet, here this woman was. She'd smacked Brianna over the head with a hammer—probably more than once—and now she was standing over her with an axe.

The unthinkable seemed to be unavoidable.

Brianna tried to scramble away. The sides of her bare feet scraped against the floor until her shoulders struck the wall behind her. There was nowhere left to go. The room had just one door and Brianna had no way to reach it. What appeared to be an axe murderer stood between her and freedom.

She screamed, but the only noises that made the distance from her throat through the tape over her mouth were long, desperate groans of agony.

"Hnnnnn. Hnn. Hnnnnn."

"That's a good game. I like it. You hum the harmony, I'll play the melody. But maybe another time. I'm a little busy right now."

She swung up the axe, caught the haft with her other hand, and took a step forward.

Brianna's eyes widened in horror. A tear rolled down her dust-encrusted cheek.

The woman stopped. "I'm being mean, aren't I? You don't deserve this."

Brianna shook her head, her cheekbone rubbing against the floor.

"Oh, but you do. And you should know why. You should know who's about to make you shorter by a whole head, and why I'm about to do it." She paused and gripped the axe tighter. "My name is Lisa Kerne. Does any part of that name ring a bell?"

Brianna trembled. She had no idea who this woman was. She didn't recognize the name from college or school or any of the bars she went to with her housemates on Saturday nights. Nothing made sense.

Hope flickered for an instant, as brief as the spark on a cigarette lighter. Maybe this psycho had made a mistake. Maybe as soon as she realized she'd gotten the wrong person, she'd let her go with an apology for all the trouble she'd caused.

The flash died as soon as Lisa Kerne spoke again.

"You don't know me, huh? How disappointing. I should be insulted, considering how much harm your family has done to mine. Well, I know who you are, Brianna Yates. You're Hagen Yates's sister."

Brianna's breathing hastened into short, quick gasps that sucked the smell of the duct tape over her mouth deep into her nostrils. There was no mistake. This Lisa Kerne knew who she was. And she was here because of Hagen.

A burst of hot anger exploded in Brianna's chest.

Hagen was supposed to protect her. He was supposed to look after her. But now she was here, tied up in a basement, lying at the feet of a madwoman with an axe.

And where was he?

It wasn't fair. Whatever Hagen had done, this wasn't her fault.

The woman dropped to her haunches and drew her face closer to Brianna's. "Your brother, together with his friends in the FBI, killed my father. They murdered him in cold blood. All he wanted to do was create a world fit for music. Fit for me. And the FBI killed him."

She pushed herself to her feet and rested the axe on her shoulder like a baseball bat.

"Enough. It's time to take my revenge. *Off with her head!*"

40

"Hagen!"

Stella raced toward the music center, but Hagen was too fast and too far ahead. A wide set of stairs stretched across the entrance, and he reached the top of them as Stella reached the bottom step. Hagen yanked open the door and disappeared into the building.

Stella shouted after him. "Hagen!"

Behind her came Ander, giving Slade the blow-by-blow as he ran. "He's gone inside, sir. Yes, Hagen. And he's mad as hell."

Stella leapt up the stairs and threw the door open. The foyer was empty. Where the hell had he gone?

Ander spoke from behind her. "I'll check the offices."

As Ander disappeared into the music center's administration rooms, Stella opened the door of the auditorium.

The hall was almost entirely dark. Emergency lights bathed the huge space in eerie yellow light. Two signs on the far wall indicated fire exits in bold red. No one was onstage or anywhere in sight.

In the gloom, Stella could just make out the shapes of the

musicians' chairs, a thin forest of music stands. The solid form of the piano dominated the left side of the stage. A line of white light penetrated the back of the stage from the wings.

Propping open the door with the cast on her arm, Stella listened.

The door creaked against her shoulder. The air-conditioning hummed. Somewhere over by the offices, a door opened and creaked shut. But in the auditorium, all was still.

Stella fished into her pocket for her phone and called Stacy. The line didn't even finish ringing once before Stacy answered. Her voice was no louder than a whisper. "Backstage corridor. Stage right."

Stacy disconnected the call.

Stella relayed the message to Ander and ran down the stairs toward the stage. As soon as the door closed, the usually warm auditorium was plunged into a smoky twilight.

She stumbled over the steps, her hip brushing the edge of the seats.

C'mon, don't fall and break your other arm.

With one hand guiding her, she reached the small set of stairs leading to the stage and ran up them. A music stand clattered to the floor as she pushed between the chairs to the wing.

Stacy's fast reply and the quick hang-up unnerved Stella. She didn't dare call again, but she wasn't sure what she'd find in the backstage corridor, stage right.

If she was lucky, she'd bump into Hagen and persuade him to get the hell out of here.

If she was unlucky, she'd run right into Lisa Kerne, armed and ready to kill, waiting in the shadows for the FBI.

Stella drew her weapon. Just in case.

She slipped into the wing. A corridor stretched the length of the stage, a single line of fluorescent bulbs turning the walls a drab brown. Stella had been here before.

The large dressing room stood at the end of the corridor, but halfway down the passage was an opening. A figure disappeared down a flight of stairs and out of sight, and all Stella could hear were footsteps tapping steadily downward.

Hagen.
The basement.

She booked it down the hall.

When she heard him scream, "Brianna!" she picked up the pace, sailing toward the passageway.

Stacy's voice came next, with an authority Stella hadn't heard from her before.

"FBI. I said, *put it down*. Do it now!"

That wasn't the voice of a third cello or new recruit. It was the voice of a determined law enforcement officer expecting to be obeyed.

Lisa was there. They'd found her. They'd found them both.

Without waiting to check whether Ander was following, Stella turned and leapt down the stairs, taking them two at a time and ignoring the stabbing pain in her ribs with each movement. A metal door stood wide open at the bottom of the stairwell.

With a final jump, Stella was in the doorway. She stretched her arms forward, her gun raised. Her lame arm offered support.

The room was dark—half of the lightbulbs were burned out—but her eyes had already adjusted to the gloom. A figure lay against the wall on her right side, their legs bound and their arms pulled behind their back. A form crouched alongside it. Stella recognized Hagen's muscular but slim silhouette instantly.

She stepped to her left to get a better view of the big picture.

Hagen tugged at something on the figure's face. It ripped. *Tape.*

Then he laid a hand on their cheek. His shoulders shook. "Brianna…"

Everything in the room seemed to have come to a sudden stop.

Stacy stood directly in front of Stella, a gun aimed at Lisa Kerne, who was backed against the far wall, hands by her sides.

Lisa looked over Stacy's shoulder, a bitter smile on her face. "Agent Knox, so glad you could join us."

Like father, like daughter. This was a killer encore if she'd ever seen one.

She shifted her gaze back to the new FBI officer in front of her. Neither of them moved. With Stacy blocking most of her view, Stella could only make out the left side of Lisa's face.

"Brianna." Hagen's voice was soft, pleading.

Brianna's head rose from the floor.

She coughed. "Hagen? Took you long enough."

Hagen pulled her into his arms.

Relief swept through Stella. Brianna was alive, and she was okay. They'd found her in time.

Hagen peeled the tape off Brianna's wrists and ankles.

Stacy, however, was the one in control of the room.

"I said *drop it*! Do it now!"

Stella couldn't see what Lisa Kerne was holding.

With one hand still on the grip of her gun and with a vein pulsing in her temple, Stella stepped deeper into the room, shifting around Stacy's left flank, away from Hagen and Brianna. She slipped around until she could see both Lisa and Stacy more clearly.

The pianist's arms hung straight down, but her right hand

held what looked to be a stick. As Stella crept farther in, she made out the head of the axe at the bottom of the haft.

The weapon that had cut through Jane Lin's neck hung at the pianist's side.

Stella's fingers closed around the grip of her gun.

"Do as she says, Lisa. It's over. You're done."

Lisa turned toward Stella. The axe twitched by her knee, the blade rocking back and forth. "I wonder which way I ought to go."

Stella nearly smiled. *"Careful. She's stark raving mad."* She knew her *Alice in Wonderland* quotes too.

The pair were more than a pace away from Lisa Kerne, so no matter how fast Lisa moved or how quickly she swung that axe, she wouldn't make it before both Stella and Stacy got off a shot.

Lisa must have reached the same conclusion. She sighed. "Beaten by a third cello. So *embarrassing*."

The axe clattered to the concrete floor. Stella relaxed her grip on her weapon. She exhaled with relief.

"Put your hands where we can see them, Lisa. Hold them up," Stacy ordered.

Lisa Kerne lifted her arms and spread her fingers like she was about to pounce onto her keyboard and beat out the opening to Beethoven's Fifth, not be read her Miranda Rights. Stacy's weapon was still aimed at her heart.

Stella holstered her gun and reached behind her belt for her handcuffs. She stepped behind Lisa.

Over the murderer's shoulder, Stella saw Brianna rubbing the circulation back into her legs. Hagen climbed to his feet.

Though she could only see Lisa in profile, she watched as the madwoman found Hagen's eyes and flashed him a sardonic smile.

Somehow, before Stella could even compute what was

happening, with a draw straight out of the Old West, Hagen's weapon was in his hand, its muzzle aimed at Lisa.

Lisa's smile widened. "Do it."

Stella yanked Lisa back, dragging her to the ground while, simultaneously, Stacy dove, launching into Hagen's side. Her shoulder knocked his arm upward, shifting the gun toward the ceiling.

A flash of light flooded the room.

Bam.

Plaster dropped from the ceiling, sprinkling dust onto Stella's face. Pain burst through her ribs as Lisa fell against her. The same ribs that had taken a blow when Hagen had shot Boris Kerne were getting the brunt of his rash actions once again. And once again, his gun had gone off. Hagen had opened fire. Stella managed to keep ahold of Lisa's cuffed hands and roll her toward the wall.

Lisa lay on the ground beside her. She was laughing, a wild, manic laugh that was interrupted by random bursts of, *"Off with her head!"*

In the corner, Stacy still had Hagen's arm pinned to the wall, his gun still pointing at the ceiling.

We're all mad here.

41

Hagen perched on the edge of the stage in the auditorium of the Kentwood Philharmonic. A strange tiredness had crept over him, as though a lifetime of fear had been drained from his body over the course of an hour. He barely had the strength to stand.

In the front row, directly in front of Hagen's feet, Brianna sat sandwiched between Slade and Stacy. Brianna's bare feet were on the seat, her knees pulled into her chest, as though she were curled into the corner of her sofa watching a rom-com with her roommates on a cold winter evening. The sight warmed Hagen. Maybe this experience wouldn't leave a deep scar on her, after all. Perhaps she could return to her life and leave this mess in the past.

In the row behind her, a paramedic wrapped a bandage around the crown of her head.

Rubbing the red marks on her wrists, Brianna explained in a quiet, halting voice how she'd planned to cram in some extra studying that morning before spending the day at her sister's ranch. She'd opened the door in response to an urgent knock, offered help to a woman who seemed to need it, and had taken a blow to the side of her head as thanks for her generosity and public spirit.

The account made Hagen wince. He should have told her to be more careful. If he'd warned her against opening the door to strangers, told Brianna about the case they were investigating, maybe none of this would have happened. Blame burrowed inside him, even as he knew, without a shadow of a doubt, that Brianna would have ignored his warning when a woman came knocking on her door in need of help. That was just the way she was.

Brianna continued, explaining that she had no recollection of the journey from her home to Kentwood. She didn't know the route they'd taken, nor had she heard anything her captor might have said until she woke up on a concrete floor, bound and gagged and with a headache that still pounded, despite the painkiller the paramedic had offered.

Stacy scratched away at a notebook. "When you regained consciousness alone and in the dark, you must have been terrified."

Brianna hugged her knees tighter. "I wasn't sure I'd woken up at first. I couldn't move or see anything. The only reason I knew I wasn't dead was the pain. My wrists. My ankles. My head most of all."

Hagen's chest tightened. He tried to will himself to relax. This wasn't his sister talking. This was just another victim, another member of the public who'd been assaulted and abducted. And almost killed. The kind of victim he'd been running into far too often lately.

Brianna touched her forehead as the paramedic adjusted the bandage. "The only thing that kept me going as I lay there, the only thing that made me sure my brother was going to rescue me, was the music."

Stacy lifted her pen from her notebook. "The music?"

"I could hear music. While I was down there. Classical. I

figured if I could hear it, there were people nearby. And as long as there were people nearby, I'd be okay. Hagen would find me. I was sure he would."

She looked up at the stage, and a warmth spread through Hagen's chest, loosening the cold tightness that had gripped him as he listened to his sister. Brianna had believed in him. Despite all that had happened, she still believed in him.

And yet, her confirmation of his responsibility anchored him in place like concrete, heavy and solid.

They all looked at him now. Every one of them. He'd failed his family when his dad had died. He couldn't fail them again.

Slade's phone beeped. He checked the screen, then patted the arm of the chair. "Thank you, Brianna. You've been a huge help. Stacy, looks like Lisa Kerne's already on her way to the cells, so why don't you and the paramedic take Brianna to the ambulance to finish her treatment? I'll send Hagen to join you in a moment. I just need to have a word with him first."

Stacy slipped her notebook into her jacket pocket and stood. She hesitated for a moment before coming to a decision. "I'll come by tomorrow to pick up my cello. I'm sure it will be safe here until then."

She didn't look sure as she waited for the paramedic to apply the last touches to the bandage, but once Brianna had unfolded herself from the chair, Stacy stretched her fingers over the small of Brianna's back. Slowly, they made their way up past the empty seats to the exit. When they reached the top of the steps, Brianna stopped at the door and turned back toward Hagen.

He gave her a small nod, and she smiled. Her warm eyes lingered on him for a moment, and that look was all the thanks he needed. It was more than he felt he deserved. The door swung closed behind her.

Slade leaned back in his seat and steepled his fingers. For a moment, he said nothing, then he lifted his chin and looked directly at Hagen.

"What happened?"

"I couldn't stay at the ranch anymore, so I came down here to see if I could help. You called to say that Stacy had lost sight of Kerne, so I went in to look for her and find Brianna. I saw Stacy heading down the stairs and followed. When I got there, she had Lisa in her sights, and Brianna was tied up on the floor. While Stacy kept her gun on Lisa, I made sure Brianna was okay."

Slade waited until Hagen was finished before standing, filling the narrow space between the bottom of the stage and the first row of seats.

Hagen was a good couple of inches taller than his boss, and the height of the stage gave him another three feet. But he was sitting, and when Slade put his hands on his hips and filled his chest, the special supervisory agent seemed to double in size.

"In all my years, Hagen, I don't think I've ever heard such a load of bullcrap from one person in one place. You had no business being here. Your place was on the ranch with your sister and your mother, not running around in here like a chicken with its head cut off!"

Slade glared at him. His nostrils flared and the lines in his forehead creased deep enough to hold a nickel.

Hagen had never heard Slade talk like that to anyone, not even in interrogations.

Surely, Slade understood why he'd come.

Surely, he'd have done the same.

Anyone would have.

Slade's eyes flashed. "What happened in that room? Why is there a bullet lodged in that ceiling? A bullet from your damn gun. *Again.*"

Hagen exhaled. There were two answers to that question. The simple one, which also had the benefit of being true, was that Stacy had knocked his arm into the wall, and as his fingers had clenched in response, he'd squeezed the trigger.

But that didn't explain why his finger was on the trigger in the first place. The answer to that question, he'd rather not give. And so far, Slade hadn't asked him, not in so many words.

Behind him, Stella's footsteps pattered softly toward the piano. She took her place on the stool, a cup of hot chocolate from the vending machine steaming in her hand.

The distraction made Hagen almost smile. He'd seen the vending machine in the dressing room and had known that as long as they'd have to wait, Stella wouldn't miss the opportunity to try a cup.

She must have left Ander downstairs in the basement rehearsal room, telling the forensic team where to swab and what to take. She touched her ribs and winced, but as she sipped from her cup, confidence warmed Hagen's chest. He was no longer alone. It was no longer just him and that horrible moment in the practice room. He had Stella with him too.

Hagen closed his eyes. And the auditorium, Slade, and Stella Knox all faded away. There was nothing but blackness and relief and ease. When he opened his eyes again, he imagined he was in court, addressing a judge. The room's acoustics sent his words across the hall, even as he kept his voice calm and even.

"Once I'd seen the victim was alive and healthy, I pulled my weapon to support Stacy and Stella in persuading Lisa Kerne to surrender."

"By shooting her?"

"Shooting her? No, I wasn't going to shoot her, not unless she gave me a reason to."

Slade glared at him. Hagen didn't move. He wasn't lying. He'd had a good reason to shoot Lisa Kerne from the moment he knew she'd taken Brianna. For a second, he'd just been blind to all the reasons not to shoot her. The blindness frightened him. He didn't want his memory to go there again.

His superior's face remained impassive. "Stacy believed you were about to shoot Lisa Kerne. She said the suspect had dropped her weapon and was preparing to surrender when you drew *your* weapon and aimed it at the suspect. Hagen, Stacy thought you were going to kill Kerne."

Hagen sighed. The new girl had a big mouth.

"She's new. She overreacted. I don't recall if I drew my weapon before or after the suspect dropped the axe, but I didn't intend to use lethal force unless life was at risk." He paused. That was more than he'd wanted to say, but it was everything he *should* say. That intention was also what he wanted to believe. From now on, it *would* be true. "At least one of us needed to keep a weapon trained on her while the other cuffed her. I don't know what was going through Stacy's head, but the discharge didn't happen until she barreled into me and knocked my arm into the wall."

"She says she was preventing you from shooting Lisa Kerne."

Hagen looked directly into Slade's eyes. "She made a mistake. It happens. You learn, you move on."

Slade stepped back. He rubbed his temples with one hand and paced in front of the seats. "This is all I need. There will be another investigation. This is the second case in a row you've discharged your weapon."

Hagen pushed off the stage, landing with a solid thud behind his boss. "Just a minute. Boris Kerne had already opened fire when I shot him."

Slade spun around. "Tell that to the investigators."

"I did!"

"And now you've got something else to tell them. Dammit, Hagen, I can't afford to lose an agent. If you get hauled over the coals for this…"

Hagen sighed. He didn't want Slade to finish his sentence either. He could take a suspension. Heck, a few days off the job while Stella was pinned down with another case could be just what he needed. But if he was fired…that was a whole other scenario.

Surely, an investigation wouldn't go that far. It couldn't.

Slade flopped into one of the seats. He looked ready to leave this world of killers and discharged weapons behind him, to relax and enjoy a performance.

Hagen didn't share that relief. Horrific and terrifying as Lisa Kerne's threats had been for him and his family, he had done what he needed to do, what he should always do. His family had been threatened, and he'd dealt with that threat and neutralized it. Whether he'd be as successful next time, he couldn't say. But as long as he stayed on this case, he wouldn't have to think about the dangers of the next one.

Slade stretched his legs and let the seat take his weight.

"There's nothing to do now. The investigators will come sniffing again, and we'll have to jump off that bridge when we get to it. Or find someone to throw off it." He sighed. "I've told Martin we got the woman who killed his sister. I think it helped. He didn't say much, but I got the impression the news will help him heal."

Hagen took a deep breath. He longed for the chance to have that kind of healing. "I'm sure it will."

42

Stella took a long sip of her hot chocolate and let the cup hide her face. She'd seen the axe in Lisa Kerne's hand.

She'd also heard the solid *thunk* when it dropped to the floor. Only then had Hagen drawn his weapon, when Lisa Kerne was unarmed, and Stacy had her well-covered.

Slade held his gaze on Hagen for a moment before turning toward the piano. "Stella, with me."

Stella placed her cup on the floor next to the piano stool and followed Slade into the wings.

"You heard all that." He spoke in a whisper. "Anything you want to add?"

Stella hesitated. She wasn't sure what to tell him. Hagen had reached for his gun, Stacy had dived at him, and his weapon had gone off. Those were the facts. As for Hagen's intentions, she had no more than suspicions and doubts.

"No, sir. Not really. I saw Hagen pull his weapon, and when Stacy leapt toward him, the gun discharged. When it did, I figured I needed to protect Lisa Kerne from a second possible discharge."

"So you think Stacy endangered the life of the suspect?"

"I...I wouldn't..." Stella wasn't sure what to say. "I was just concerned about the possibility of another discharge. I didn't know...that is, I wouldn't say Stacy risked anyone's life. I'm sure she did what she thought was right."

Slade scratched his forehead and sighed. "I have no idea what to make of that. I'll try to support them both, but if investigators decide to throw the book at either one, I don't know how much protection I can give. And that would be a real shame. Stacy's brand new to our office and very promising, and you and Hagen are about the best we've got. Dammit." He pointed at her ribs. "How you doing there?"

The pain was sharp but not as bad as the initial injury. "I'll live."

Slade cocked his head toward the stage. "Good. Go finish your drink and get out of here. I'll see how Ander's getting on. And tell Hagen to head to the ambulance. His sister's waiting."

Stella waited for Slade to disappear into the passageway and down the stairs. She felt sorry for Stacy. The new girl really had only done what she'd thought was right, and she'd put herself at risk too. There was some real courage behind her formal, sometimes-nervous exterior.

And Hagen's troubles just kept on coming.

Stella walked back onto the stage and stopped in surprise. Mac was at the top of the stairs. Surrounded by empty seats, she looked tiny, her white-blond hair standing out against the auditorium's black walls. She seemed to take a moment to recognize she was in the right place before skipping down the steps and jumping onto the stage.

"Mac!" Stella called. "What are you doing here?"

Mac pushed her hands into her pockets. She was wearing a pair of loose-fitting black slacks that stopped above her ankles. Standing in front of the empty orchestra seats, she looked ready to give a TED Talk. On realizing she was front and center, she scampered downstage and sat down in front of Hagen, one leg hanging below the edge of the platform.

"I...I heard you guys caught Lisa Kerne. I just wanted to see how everyone was doing. This case was personal..."

As Stella returned to the piano stool, Hagen nodded and dropped into the chair opposite Mac. He looked as exhausted as he did relieved.

Whatever had happened in that basement, whatever Stacy had thought and reported, whatever he'd intended to do, and whatever the investigation would conclude was for the birds now. This case was over, and Hagen's sister would soon be home. Nothing else mattered.

"Yeah, we got her." His lips had formed the tiniest of smiles. "There's a forensic team downstairs with Ander doing their...stuff. They'll go over her car when they're done there. But yeah, it's over. Brianna's a bit bashed up, but she's gonna be okay."

Mac grinned at him. She had a warm smile that reached her eyes and made them twinkle in the auditorium's overhead lights. So happy to learn that Brianna was safe.

She kicked her leg. "That's awesome. What a relief."

Stella remembered Slade's instructions. "Hey, Hagen, Slade says you're free to go. Get yourself up to that ambulance. Your sister's waiting."

Hagen acknowledged the order, but he didn't move. His hands curled over the ends of the armrests, and he remained in his place. As relieved as he appeared at the end of this case, now that it was over, he also seemed to want to hold onto it and keep it close. At least for a little longer.

Mac climbed to her feet. "Hey, Stella, got something for you."

About Joel?

"Oh, yeah? Whatcha got?" She attempted to keep her voice neutral.

Mac crossed the stage to the piano and waited for Stella to sidle across the stool to give her room.

She lowered her voice. "I've got a lead on your informant."

Hagen frowned and his knuckles whitened on the sides of his chair.

Stella winced. The acoustics in the auditorium of the Kentwood Philharmonic were better than Mac must have expected. Even though she'd spoken quietly, her voice must have carried to Hagen.

Rising to his feet and making his way down the front row of seats toward the piano, Hagen kept his eyes on Stella.

"You've got an informant? For your father's murder?"

Stella lifted her cup from the floor and took another sip of the hot chocolate. It was cool now, but she didn't want Hagen to see her irritation at Mac's slip. She composed herself and lowered the cup.

"'Informant' is strong. I got a call. From someone who said he knew my dad back in the day. And knows who killed him."

Hagen's eyes narrowed. Stella could almost see the trust slipping away.

"Is that right? He give a name?"

"No. That was why I didn't say anything. He didn't give anything of any use to anyone. There are plenty of people out there who knew my dad, and I assume at least one of them knows who killed him. This guy didn't tell me anything I didn't know already."

Hagen stopped at the audience seat closest to the piano.

He looked like a subscriber to the philharmonic waiting for a soloist to entertain him. Stella was still on the stool, her elbows resting on her thighs. Either she'd play or she wouldn't. But all the control was in her hands. And right now, she was holding onto that power and keeping it close. She wasn't sure what Hagen would do with the information once he got it, and the thought both frightened and saddened her.

Mac gave Stella's shoulder a friendly nudge with her own. "I've got something you don't know about that informant. Either of you."

Stella's gaze slid from her cup to Mac. She couldn't tell Mac to keep it to herself, not with Hagen just standing there. She bit her lower lip, then gave her friend a small nod. "Go on."

Mac took a deep breath. "The call did come from a burner, as you'd expect. But when I looked at the call records, I was able to see that the caller wasn't the most careful guy in the world. Looks like he used the phone more than once, and from the same area."

Stella nodded. "You have an address?"

"I think so. I triangulated the caller's position from local cell towers and found three houses that fell within the area. I looked at their ownership records. One of them is owned by a local teacher. She's been at the same school for almost thirty years. No law enforcement connections as far as I could tell."

Hagen tapped the edge of the stage. "And the others?"

"One of the other houses changed ownership between the dates of the first and second calls from the burner. I can't rule out the calls being made from that house, but I think it's unlikely."

"Find something good about the third house?"

Stella glanced at Hagen. He sounded impatient, irritated at Mac's slow response.

Mac ignored his testiness. "Yeah. I did. It's owned by a

cop who serves on the Memphis police force." Mac brought out her phone and opened a map. "It's right here."

Mac's finger pointed to a small house at the end of a cul-de-sac. Hagen stared at the screen. When he looked up, his eyes met Stella's.

They both had an address to get to.

43

Sis rested her arm against the trunk of an elm tree and watched blue-and-red lights flash against the wall of the concert hall. They looked so pretty, those lights—like fireworks that would burn forever.

Whenever something had gone wrong, whenever someone like her decided to do things *their* way instead of the way someone else decided was the right way, those lights would sparkle and warn the world.

Alert! Someone's breaking our rules. Now watch what we do to them.

Sis lifted the brown paper bag and took a swig from the beer bottle inside.

She was standing in the small park opposite the Kentwood Philharmonic. The time was closing in on midnight, and the park was empty.

This was exactly the kind of place kids would come to toss a ball around in the afternoons and families would sit and picnic on the weekends. And as soon as the sun set, a place where teenagers would find a bench to neck in the evenings. Though maybe not. Round here in Kentwood, Sis was pretty sure people had giant yards of their own where they could do all those things if they wanted.

But for now, the park was empty. And in the darkness under the tree, Sis could stand and watch the commotion without being seen.

As she took another sip of beer, two figures clad in white suits emerged from the building, clutching what looked like large sandwich bags. They placed the bags in the back of a van before turning and climbing the stairs again, passing a familiar figure on his way down.

The figure stopped at the back of an ambulance, lowered his head, and climbed inside. A paramedic closed the doors behind him, and the ambulance set off down the road, lights flashing but sirens off.

Sis muttered to herself. "Guess your condition isn't too bad, huh, Hagen Yates? You look like you're alive and well. At least for now."

She took her phone from her pocket and made a call.

The voice that answered was deep and warm and as welcoming as a hot drink on a cold day. "Hey, hun. Didn't expect to hear from you tonight."

"Is that right? Does that mean I caught you at your lover's?"

He chuckled. "Now, you know I'd never do that. I'd bring her right here if I knew you weren't at home. Both of them. Together."

Sis laughed. The lights on the building flashed red. "And you know what I'd do to them if I thought even one word of that could possibly be true. And to you."

"Uh-huh. You know there's only you, honey. There could only ever be you."

"That's right. And don't you ever forget it."

The door of the concert hall opened again. The unmistakable form of Stella Knox came out this time, one arm still in a cast. Seeing her in the flesh after spending so much time watching her on the surveillance camera gave Sis a little spark of excitement, like passing a celebrity on the sidewalk.

Sis lowered the phone and muttered to herself. "Maybe I should ask you for an autograph, Stella Knox. Or perhaps a selfie."

Stella was accompanied by Mackenzie Drake, the computer nerd Sis had recently been researching. She'd seen the small woman with the white-blond hair on the surveillance video and knew that she and Stella seemed to have a pretty close relationship. The pair climbed into a car and were soon driving away from the building in the direction of the city. Sis watched them go.

She lifted her phone again. "You know what I'm doing right now, hun?"

"I assume you're in your trailer, thinking about me."

Sis smiled. "Well, you'd be wrong. I'm outside a concert hall in Kentwood where the FBI have just finished making an arrest. The place is a mess. The killer they were after targeted one of their own, the lucky bastard. Must have been a real pleasure for her."

His soft chuckle curled her toes. "Lucky but stupid. If the FBI are there, then she got caught, didn't she? We...*you*...are a lot smarter than that. Least, I hope you're being smarter than that."

"Oh, don't you worry about me now. I've got my head screwed on. Which is more than I can say for that woman's first victim. Real mean streak, she had. Nasty. I kinda liked her, even if she was dumb enough to let them catch her."

"Don't underestimate them." His voice was low and urgent. "You don't have to be dumb to get caught by the FBI. You just have to make a mistake. One is all it takes. They'll be onto you faster than summer flies on a plate of barbeque."

The edge of Sis's lip rose. Now they were getting somewhere. That warning was what she wanted to hear. It stank of fear, and she knew how to make fear work for her.

"That's right. And that's why we gotta move now. We should have done this earlier, but better late than never. They're off balance. Hagen Yates is still traumatized about his sister, and who the hell knows what's going through that Stella Knox's head? We take them out now, we're done. It's over."

"Hey now, just a minute—"

"Screw your minutes! We don't have a second, let alone a minute. Soon, they'll all be up and focused again, and we'll have missed the best chance we've ever had to put this whole stupid mess to bed once and for all. I can deal with the Knox girl now and wait for Hagen to get back from comforting his baby sister. They won't see me coming."

"Hush. You said not on the phone. Never on the phone. Are you crazy?"

That made her laugh. "Yeah, I'm crazy." Sis turned away from the music center and strode farther into the park. She lowered her voice until it was little more than a hiss. "I've been crazy since I got here, ever since I took over from that no-good idiot brother of mine."

"Now, hun, I—"

"Don't 'now, hun' me. This whole thing should have been over a long time ago. Instead, all I do is sit here and watch and wait like some kinda Peeping Tom. If I don't get to act soon, I'm gonna…heck, I don't know what I'm gonna do, but it's going to be big, and it's going to be very, very bloody."

"All right, all right. Just keep your voice down. I'll go and talk to The Officer. Maybe I can—"

"I've tried. He doesn't listen. I'm telling you, this isn't the time for talking anymore. This is the time to act."

"I know, I know. You're right."

Confidence pulsed through Sis, strong and hard. "Damn right, I'm right."

"But don't."

Sis stopped walking. "Don't what?"

"Don't act. That's what."

Sis rolled back her head and stared at the heavens. The Big Dipper arced above her, its giant spoon ready to scoop the scum from the surface of the world and hold it high.

"But you just—"

"I know what I just said, and I know what will happen if you disobey The Officer. And so do you. Better than anyone. That guy, man, he doesn't give a shit. He'll give the order to take you out, and he'll give it to me just for the sheer fun of it. Hold on. You've spoken to him on the phone. I'm down here. I'll go talk to him face to face. You just *wait*."

Sis hung up and jammed her phone back into her pocket. With one long chug, she emptied the forty, leaned back, and hurled it into the darkness.

Something wasn't right.

The time for watching was over.

44

R*rrrring.*
Stella stretched her good arm toward the alarm clock. Her fingers landed on the corner of the bed.

Rrrrring.

She mumbled, summoning the energy to push the words out of her mouth. "Jeez, will you shut up already?"

Rrrrring.

The answer, apparently, was "no." Stella's alarm clock would not shut up.

She pushed herself up. The cast covering the bottom of her hand landed on top of the clock's bell, killing the noise entirely. She flopped back onto the bed and closed her eyes.

No. She was probably setting off too late. She needed to get to the informant before Hagen, who was definitely on his way already. Mornings were not a chore for him the way they were for her.

"Ugh. Hagen."

The image of the basement rehearsal room flashed back into her head. The sight of Brianna trussed up on the floor. Lisa Kerne's impassive face.

Hagen drawing his weapon, aiming.

Stacy darting toward Hagen. Stella covering Lisa Kerne.

The memory made Stella nauseous.

Maybe what Hagen had told Slade was the truth.

Maybe he really was going to cover Lisa while she and Stacy searched and cuffed her.

But suspicion twisted Stella's guts.

He *would* have shot an unarmed suspect.

Despite what he'd told Slade, despite what *she'd* told their boss, a voice at the back of her head, too loud to ignore, told her Hagen would've shot Lisa Kerne.

Unarmed. Having surrendered. He'd have shot her if Stacy hadn't stopped him.

He might even have hit his target with a second shot if Stella hadn't shoved Lisa Kerne out of the way.

She swung her legs out of bed.

No. He wouldn't do that.

She wanted to believe Stacy was overreacting. That she had been wrong. Hagen was innocent. She wanted to believe she pushed Lisa out of the way for nothing.

Stella really did want to believe all of that. But doubt gnawed at her insides with teeth as sharp and persistent as a rat's.

Her alarm clock had fallen on its back. Stella dragged it back into place before hopping out of bed.

She washed and dressed as quickly as she could with one hand. There wouldn't be much traffic on a Sunday morning, but the drive to Memphis would still take the best part of three hours.

She'd pick up a hot chocolate from the café downstairs and drink it on the way.

She had to get to Memphis before Hagen. If he reached the informant's house before she did, if he…

She imagined a dead, faceless police officer lying on the ground, a bullet in his head, while Hagen stood over him, smoke trailing from the end of his gun.

Stella shuddered.

He wouldn't do that.

And yet, here she was, grabbing her purse and reaching for her keys, racing Hagen to the informant. Because she didn't trust him.

If his sisters and mother made him stay longer at the ranch, she still had a chance.

She lifted the paper towel roll on her kitchen counter and found her keys. Tugging the charger out of her phone, Stella explained her turmoil to her goldfish. "You know, Scoot. I'm supposed to be able to trust Hagen, and yet I'm scared to death he's going to get there before me. Fine partners we make, huh?"

Her goldfish opened and closed his mouth but had nothing to say.

"Yeah, exactly."

She slipped her phone into her pocket and headed for the door. The café would just be opening, so if there was no line, she'd be on the road in little more than five minutes. She couldn't do better than that.

Her pocket vibrated. Stella stopped with her hand on the door and retrieved her phone.

Chloe.

At seven twenty on a Sunday morning.

Stella took the call.

"Hey, Stella. Didn't wake you, did I?"

Stella harrumphed. "Sadly, no."

"That's what I figured. Listen, a friend's discovered a body at his gym. Looks like we're about to get another case."

The End
To be continued...

Thank you for reading.
All of the *Stella Knox Series* books can be found on Amazon.

ACKNOWLEDGMENTS

How does one properly thank everyone involved in taking a dream and making it a reality? Here goes.

In addition to our families, whose unending support provided the foundation for us to find the time and energy to put these thoughts on paper, we want to thank the editors who polished our words and made them shine.

Many thanks to our publisher for risking taking on two newbies and giving us the confidence to become bona fide authors.

More than anyone, we want to thank you, our readers, for sharing your most important asset, your time, with this book. We hope with all our hearts we made it worthwhile.

Much love,
Mary & Stacy

ABOUT THE AUTHOR

Mary Stone

Mary Stone lives among the majestic Blue Ridge Mountains of East Tennessee with her two dogs, four cats, a couple of energetic boys, and a very patient husband.

As a young girl, she would go to bed every night, wondering what type of creature might be lurking underneath. It wasn't until she was older that she learned that the creatures she needed to most fear were human.

Today, she creates vivid stories with courageous, strong heroines and dastardly villains. She invites you to enter her world of serial killers, FBI agents but never damsels in distress. Her female characters can handle themselves, going toe-to-toe with any male character, protagonist or antagonist.

Discover more about Mary Stone on her website.
www.authormarystone.com

Stacy O'Hare

Growing up in West Virginia, most of the women in Stacy O'Hare's family worked in the medical field. Stacy was no exception and followed in their footsteps, becoming a nurse's aid. It wasn't until she had a comatose patient she became attached to and made up a whole life story about—with a past as an FBI agent included—that she discovered her love of stories. She started jotting them down, and typing them out, and expanding them when she got off shift. Somehow, they turned into a book. Then another. Now, she's over the moon to be releasing her first series.

Connect with Mary Online

- facebook.com/authormarystone
- goodreads.com/AuthorMaryStone
- bookbub.com/profile/3378576590
- pinterest.com/MaryStoneAuthor

Made in the USA
Coppell, TX
30 September 2024